RIVERS *of* THIRST

Stories of Partitions, Borders and Exile

JOGINDER PAUL

Edited by Sukrita Paul Kumar and Rushaan Kumar

SPEAKING TIGER BOOKS
125A, Ground Floor, Shahpur Jat
New Delhi – 110049

Published in English by Speaking Tiger Books 2024

ISBN: 978-93-5447-902-1

10 9 8 7 6 5 4 3 2 1

Typeset in Arno Pro by SŪRYA, New Delhi
Printed at PRINTWORKS, New Delhi

CONTENTS

Acknowledgements

This collection of Joginder Paul's short stories was conceived with the aim of compiling all of his Partition-related short fiction that has never before been brought together in Urdu, Hindi, nor English. In 2018, my friend from across the border, the eminent Pakistani critic and fiction writer Asif Farrukhi, provided the impetus for our selection of stories for this volume when he asked if, despite his many literary accomplishments, the Partition of India was the defining element of Joginder Paul's work. We needed to find the answer to this important provocation and we believe that it lies in the short stories chosen here.

Our heartfelt thanks to Farrukhi for agreeing to write the Introduction to this book, 'His own Way: Partition and the Fiction of Joginder Paul', and for his brilliant translations of two of the most important stories in this collection. Without his substantive contributions, this book would scarcely have been possible. We deeply regret that he is no more and that he could not see the completed version of the book. We hope it will serve as a fitting tribute to his gracious involvement.

We are indebted to the acclaimed Urdu writer Zahida Hina who, despite her ill-health, kept her word in writing for this book. A long-time admirer of Paul's writing, Zahida Apa's Afterword offers an incisive understanding of Joginder Paul's Partition stories, contextualising them within his oeuvre. Our sincere and warm thanks to her for her time and engagement with this collection.

We are immensely grateful to the collection's contributing translators who so willingly agreed to take on these stories. Thank you, Asif Farrukhi, Mohammad Asim Siddique, Sami Rafiq, Haris Qadeer, Maaz Bin Bilal and Saleem Mir. Many thanks to Naghma Zafir for her translation of Zahida Hina's Afterword, and to Priyanka Sarkar for bringing more cohesion across translations. A sincere thanks to Abu Zaheer Rabbani and Shad Naved for generously lending their expertise in Urdu to English translation and literary interpretations of Paul's writing.

The collection has benefited tremendously from our editor at Speaking Tiger, Pragya Singh's keen eye and enthusiastic vision for this manuscript. We are grateful to her, and to Ravi Singh, for taking on this project and bringing it to completion. Thanks also to Shalini Krishan, former editor at Speaking Tiger, for her involvement with the project in its early stages.

To the author, my father, who is Rushaan's grandfather, we are forever thankful for the gift of this writing through which we may momentarily meet him, again and again.

Editors' Notes

I. Forever a Refugee

Having known the author of these stories from close proximity as his daughter, I can say with absolute certainty that Joginder Paul's writing has been indelibly shaped by his own subjective experience of the Partition of India, as well as through a collective consciousness about division, displacement and exile. Paul was displaced during the Partition and had to migrate from Sialkot (now in Pakistani Punjab) to Ambala (now in Haryana, India) as a refugee in 1947. I believe he remained a refugee all his life, one who wrote fiction in order to find and relocate his bearings. In writing fiction, he created, and indeed inhabited, 'a parallel world', as he put it. All his fiction emerged from the anguish of being in exile even though he did not always engage with the phenomenon overtly. Even some of his more abstract stories, written in his 'modernist phase' evolve from an acute sense of loss, making Partition the vantage point from whence he developed his writerly self.

While some of the Partition stories collected in this volume bear witness to what Paul or many others may have experienced first-hand in 1947, there are also stories that grapple with the broader political and philosophical questions of borders and margins, ruptures and divisions, pain and loss, as also homelessness and rootedness. Traveling on foot and by truck across the border in deadly conditions, the author's experience of the Partition was a profoundly collective one. He suffered in fellowship with others—his two sisters, his parents, and hundreds of strangers—along the journey as well as in refugee camps on both sides of the border. His stories convey his deep sense of moral responsibility to create fictional characters and situations that demand from the reader an honest look at the alienation, hunger, and poverty of Partition refugees.

I ask myself why I chose to engage with Partition literature in my own scholarship, when I did not directly go through the trauma myself. Indeed, my own emotional and intellectual preoccupations were shaped by my father's yearning for his lost home(land). All through the first fifteen years of my childhood, thanks to my father, I constantly lived with the idea that we had to 'go back home' even though I was born in Nairobi and lived with my family in a perfectly comfortable house. Between my mother's Kenya and my father's India, home has often felt elusive for me as well, and it is with this sensibility that I approach Paul's Partition stories.

The stories collected here originally appeared in different anthologies in Urdu across his long writing career. As editors of this volume and as members of Paul's immediate family who carry our inheritance of loss and unbelonging, we have collected stories that we feel embody the author's orientation towards abandonment and borderlessness of body and mind.

We have also included a freshly translated excerpt from his well-known novel, *Sleepwalkers,* for the reader to get a more complete understanding of the different ways in which the author contextualises Partition experiences: the novel focuses on the mohajir, Deewane Maulavi Saab, who has carried Lucknow to Karachi in his mind. Politically drawn borders may be crossed physically perforce, but one's sense of belonging is infinitely more resistant to travel.

Over seventy-seven years after he became a refugee forever, and eight years after he reached his final resting place, we invite the reader to journey with Joginder Paul across and beyond borders.

Sukrita Paul Kumar
June 2024

II. Acts of Refusal: Reading and Translating My Grandfather

Working on this collection of my grandfather Joginder Paul's stories has compelled me to reckon with the (dis)continuities in narrative, memory, and feeling about the Partition of India between his generation and mine. The silence and narrative gaps surrounding the violent migration in the homes of survivors has been documented in Partition scholarship. There is now also considerable interest in what has come to be termed the postmemory of Partition, or the legacy of trauma, displacement, and unbelonging that has been passed down from survivors to subsequent generations. This transfer might occur through acts of remembrance and narration, but more often constitutes the emotional habitus of second and third generation descendants as we learn the grammar of loss, longing, hurt, and anger that are not our own but we nevertheless feel.

I grew up watching my grandfather write stories holed up in his dimly lit room under a whiskey-cigarette haze, while people—my mother, grandmother, guests, faraway relatives—all told stories about him. Yet, none of these stories ever ventured near the topic of his lived experience of the Partition. Neither he nor any of the other survivors in my family, that is, two other grandparents and my father, spoke about what they endured in 1947 or their first few years as refugees in India.

It was not until I was in college, around the year 2000, when I took my first ever flight to accompany my maternal grandparents to Qatar and Pakistan, that I witnessed the intensity of emotion between my grandfather and the people and places across the border. During our handful of days in Karachi, we stayed at the home of late Mohammad Ali Siddiqui-*ji*, whose family, including his children, extended so much warmth and hospitality, they immediately felt like family. That visit, my first and only visit to Pakistan, will forever be imprinted on my mind for how pivotal it was for my (un)learning about borders and murderous nationalisms. This experience is the reason why my first attempt at translating Paul's work from Urdu to English was of the first chapter of *Khwabrau* (Sleepwalkers), a Partition novel set in Karachi.

Recently my mother told me that years before our Karachi trip, Paul wrote *Khwabrau* in response to Siddiqui's complaint that he only wrote about the experiences of migrants from Pakistan to India, and never about those who were forcibly displaced in the other direction, like Siddiqui himself. What resulted from heeding this complaint became one of Paul's most acclaimed works. For me, translating a part of this novel has involved a new kind of intimacy with the author, his world, and the world of his mohajir characters. While stumbling over his Urdu phrases, poring over dictionaries, crowdsourcing the meaning and interpretation of his at once dense and playfully simple sentences, I remembered that he had been a professor of English literature for a part of his career. And he spoke Punjabi at home. Yet, he chose Urdu as his writerly language, specifically an Urdu that seems most at home in the liminal time-place of a Hindu author born in Sialkot in undivided Punjab in British India. I remembered how he would lament—no, rage—at the loss of the Urdu language to the communal and territorial binaries of Hindu/Muslim, India/Pakistan. As a refugee from Sialkot, Urdu was the medium through which he defied nationalist divisions, and performed the gesture of remembrance that brought both sides of the mohajir experience to life.

I ask myself then: what, if any, could my role or

contribution be in this context? How do I make sense of this literary, political, and emotional legacy? When I translated the chapter of *Khwabrau* three years ago, I was eager to overcome the incommensurability between Urdu and English, to make Paul's work more 'readable' for English audiences. As I have progressed with my work on this collection of stories, I have returned to their Urdu originals over and over, precisely to revive the jagged edges, the drama, and the needlepoint particularity of the author's words so that the reader may stumble, linger, and even labour to meet his characters in their own world, and on their own terms. I see now that to keep my grandfather's legacy alive, my task is not primarily to remember something I never lived through, neither can I compensate for the losses incurred as part of individual and collective forgetting of the Partition. Rather, I must refuse to let go of the language and the worlds he gave us.

Rushaan Kumar
August 2024

INTRODUCTION

His Own Way: Partition and the Fiction of Joginder Paul

Granted that he was young and alive at that hour—in homage to Wordsworth—but does Partition have to be *the* defining element when considering the sheer magnitude of Joginder Paul's literary accomplishments? As for many writers of his generation, his relationship with the Partition was not a simple one. A layered storyteller, and never short on nuance, Joginder Paul is much more than the Partition tag would permit him to be. Many of his writings emerged from his experiences of 1947, but still, he cannot be confined within his depictions of the travails that millions suffered during the Partition. His oeuvre extends to numerous other domains, and expands to span the human condition.

Diverse hands have written larger-than-life stories of the Partition, in not only Hindi and Urdu but also in English. Many of these writers have acquired fame and iconic status. But how well does Joginder Paul fare in the company of Saadat Hassan Manto, Bhisham Sahni, Krishan Chander, Krishna Sobti, and so many others? He witnessed the blood-drenched events of the Partition and wrote intensely about it, not once but repeatedly, in his decades-long writing career. Even when his narrative appears to be remote from the physical, geographical sphere of the Partition, as, for instance, when he was in Kenya and surrounded by a very different ethos, he seemed to talk and think about that event and its aftermath. The partition was an 'attitude' for him—much more than a 'theme' he chose to write about—and it marked him for his lifetime in such a manner that, at a deep level of his being, he was constantly responding to that phenomenon. With evident deliberation, he kept himself away from verdicts, pronouncements, and name-calling around how and why Partition took place. Generally, he did not turn the Partition into a cause, or a theme, or a debate, as it would have militated against his fiery, independent spirit, which he rigorously protected, so that he could always access and express the diverse dimensions of living. He avoided what he called 'surplus baggage' in a reference to Krishan Chander, a writer whom he otherwise respected. He wrote about the partition on his own terms. As a fellow storyteller, he comes across to me as an entity broken into distinct parts, each part standing as a fully integrated entity. I have read his fiction as stories within stories of the Partition and much more, encompassing themes of cultural evolution and human resilience beyond it. That is why, I intend to avoid theoretical analysis and building socio-political half-truths around his fiction. So, let me begin afresh, and draw attention to another writer, Hasan Manzar, Joginder Paul's contemporary, who travelled in the reverse direction—where one person's back faced the direction in which the other's face was turned. Manzar and Paul were not propelled by choice but pushed by a tumultuous force far beyond their control. Though their lives were mirror images, they could not have been in contact with, nor conscious of the other's position. They would barely have recognised their own situations and the grim reality of the other young men and women in those conditions. Both writers, young then, headed in the opposite directions, and yet, both refused to internalise the horrific processes of 'Othering', dehumanising, and seeing the suffering humanity as a perennial enemy. And that is what binds these two very different creative forces—they were destined to write, not just differently but in unique fashions, and yet their writings overflowed with empathy, giving their works a remarkable, transparent affinity.

Writers did not just describe the events during the 1947 Partition; their narratives also unfolded, gradually, its emotional and social aftermaths. Partition ignited the creativity that defined and expressed the subsequent happenings they described. It's ironic. The Partition, seen as a political solution to address religious aspirations and end communitarian conflicts, tragically led to devastating violence and divided people, creating two atomised societies. Differences solidified in its wake, and fuelled further divisions; partitioned minds.

Through their writings marked with a sense of permanent dislocation and displacement, Paul and Manzar painfully traced opposite paths. Paul was born in what became Pakistan and moved to live in India, while Manzar, born in India, moved during Partition with his family to the emergent Pakistan. A historical accident made them distinctive and not run-of-the-mill writers 'of' the Partition. Both writers stepped into the space vacated by the other, convincingly reflecting the lived ethos of that time. The cataclysmic events they experienced became reference points for most of their subsequent writings. In some remarkable stories, they directly confronted the phenomenon; faced the beast, as it were. Like Kurtz in Conrad's *Heart of Darkness*, they called out against something inexplicable and devastatingly beyond words, 'The Horror! The Horror!' This soul-striking horror is vividly alive in the Partition stories of Joginder Paul. But if Paul had never left Pakistan, what kind of fiction writer would he have become? What would have been his themes and creative concerns? Would he have written what he did? And if Manzar had stayed in the places Paul had moved out of, would his work have had the focus it did? Contemplating the possibility of their narratives switching places, akin to parallel train tracks that merge and diverge, reveals to me the deep entrenchment of their stories in their circumstances, which they always transcended while remaining rooted in them.

Both renowned fiction writers have carved their own place, but their names may not immediately come to mind when we reel out the names of stories and authors who have depicted the Partition. This is a paradox, considering how recurrent this theme and its offshoots are in the works of both writers. Manzar's short story 'Mal-e-Ghaneemat' (The Spoils of War) narrates the auction of household items of Hindus and Sikhs fleeing Lahore, and a young boy rummaging among toys and other trifles left behind by children of his age. He tries to imagine their lives with and without these toys. Keeping the focus away from the killings and sexual violence, this story, focussed on a seemingly mundane episode, throws the larger-than-life events that must have befallen those who have left into even sharper relief. In Paul's short story, 'Dera Baba Nanak', the question of who is a Muslim and who a Hindu is seemingly easily settled: religion is determined by the presence or absence of circumcision. The penis becomes a marker of identity, but not quite, for the protagonist is confused by this phallic identity, and in tragic irony, fails to comprehend which side he belongs to.

I met Joginder Paul once in Karachi. I had been

reading and absorbing his writings for long, and so I decided to record our conversation about his life and work. Our discussion was long, somewhat meandering, and very detailed. It was transcribed into Urdu. A shorter version was published (in English) in the Karachi-based monthly, *Newsline,* in its September 1990 issue. Paul spoke about some of the themes and stories that had preoccupied him, and remarked, 'I do not appreciate writers who catch hold of one technique and keep hacking it to death all their lives. To catch hold of life in all its variety, one has to place one's hands deep inside it, and pull out what one finds in that depth. Today, many people go around shouting that the story element has returned to the story after a spell of abstraction. But they see only the outer sequence; we cannot go back after having come forward. This whole issue of the "story element" makes no sense. A story is not merely a string of events, nor is it a description of great philosophical ideas. It comes from our experience of what we know and perceive in our bones. Anything extraneous [that is] latched onto a story becomes deadweight, even if it appears beautiful in itself.'

He said, 'The real story element lies in experience.

The right experience of knowledge becomes art. Art is superior to knowledge for precisely the reason that it includes experience. In Urdu there is one word, tajurba, which means both 'experiment' and 'experience'. We must differentiate between these two. Even the best and most daring experiment has to sink into experience, become part and parcel of it, before it can be termed creative...Literature grows old and weary if it keeps repeating the same truths. Even these truths change with the changing times and context. The writer has to catch hold of the particular truth of his age. Not only the truth, but the experience that it brings along.'

So, this was Paul's mission in his fiction. On the other side of the border, Manzar, too, was dealing with the truth of fiction in his stories. Completely independently, both wrote stories in which the sense of place prevails strongly, like an old house developing into a living character, independent of its human inhabitants, whom the home then inhabits. This brings us to Paul's short story, included in this collection, Grandmothers ('Daadiyan'), which is not directly about the events of the Partition, but describes separation, disruption, especially of families, and a life lived through memories. Manzar's story 'Ram Nawas 1946' also has a sense of place and makes the sorrow of the house in it palpable, first as a location of a family's problems, and then taking on a life of its own. The family here—the parents and their son's young wife—are adversely affected when a painful illness afflicts the son, while the household must simultaneously adjust to the presence of a woman with a dubious position, and we realise that she has been accommodated in their home by the patriarch, who is conducting an intimate relationship with her.

The house in 'Grandmothers' also has plenty of 'life' in it, perceived as a character no less than the human being who lives in it. From once a family mansion where many generations lived out fulsome lives, it has been reduced to a crumbling edifice with Grandma as its sole, obstinate inhabitant, refusing to move out. Grandma proliferates and multiplies, and maintains an ongoing dialogue with each of her many selves, all in complete harmony with each other, working hand in hand as old friends would. Joginder Paul keeps the story low-key. Its events and characters are closer to the ordinary rather than the miraculous and magical. It is this seeming ordinariness which powers the narrative. In being several persons, Grandma is simply being herself, following the numerous tasks and responsibilities she bore in a long life. As a homemaker, she feels married to the house, not to one person but to a household and its traditions. Moving out is not a possibility she can consider, for it is too big a rupture and disruption.

In the conversation Paul and I had, my questions were mostly about the changing scenario of the Urdu short story; the rising trend of symbolic and abstract, since the realistic trends were on a decline, the burgeoning fiction criticism in Urdu circles in India, and the influences all these exert on a creative writer. He used the word 'wardaat' (roughly equivalent to 'happening' in English) to describe the experience of the writer that gets transformed into fiction. I had asked him how he would define wardaat as a critical concept. He recounted for me the wardaat that resulted in 'Grandmothers': 'When this story was translated into English and read by a foreigner, he remarked at how it offered a unique cultural feature, that of not suffering from loneliness. A sense of community is inherently present, but we are, he told me, afraid of growing old and being lonely because we don't have in our imaginations the concept of community. Granny's own shadows create a community. My intention in this story was to demonstrate how one's idea of solitude is not what has been acquired through (bookish) knowledge or learnt from dictionaries. This is how solitude itself becomes a wardaat for some people...'

Joginder Paul's insistence was on writing a story as a 'happening', something akin to a live experience, not by following the popular or critically sanctioned trends. He insisted on writing a story based on his perception of its kernel of inner truth. He wished to be closer to the experience rather than accepting any formulae to write.

Now comes an unexpected twist. Going back to Joginder Paul and Hasan Manzar. Midway through their writing careers, they both visited each other's countries—which were actually their *own* countries, where they were born and grew up, but where they were now formally designated as foreigners, and required official permissions acquired through laborious processes to visit. The irony was not lost on either, as both penned their accounts of their visits. Joginder Paul's account of his journey mentions having met Hasan Manzar as his train moved towards

Hyderabad Railway Station. A more nuanced account is in his fiction, the novel *Khwabrau* (Sleepwalkers). The novel depicts a city whose people carry on with life while dreaming, lost in the memories of some city they have left behind. The continuity of the dream keeps their relationship with the past alive but does not allow them to develop any real feelings for the city they inhabit. Which city, then, is theirs? The one they dream about or the one they live in? Which part of their lives is real, the reality of the dream or the one that makes them dream? The profound symbolism is intensified by the cities being located in Pakistan and India as a consequence of the Partition and, therefore, not amenable to a visit by the majority of the residents, except in their dreams or stories of the past.

Joginder Paul wrote other accounts of his visits across the border, as did his contemporary, the Urdu writer Ramlal, who migrated to India from Pakistan. Intizar Husain also penned memoires of his multiple visits to India and in his autobiography, *Justuju Kia Hai?* (2011), recounting his trip to his childhood home in a small North Indian town. Hasan Manzar, too, wrote a travel account of his visit to Delhi where he stayed with Joginder Paul and his family. He titled it 'Kabhi Meri, Kabhi Unki Delhi', and included it in the collection, *Khak Ka Rutba,* published in 2007. Manzar's write-up is straightforward, somewhat diary-like; a rather detailed account of what he did, the people he met, and the feelings his visit evoked. Totally at home with Paul and his family, his account is a warm record with a subtext suggesting a possible role reversal, a change in identities, and so on. A sense of unease, displacement, and dispossession runs through the text.

More than a partition on bare geographical terms, this was a separation of hopes and memories; roots were wrenched away, as were longings and aspirations, and replaced with the emptiness of re-establishing homes, watching as neighbours became strangers. Joginder Paul did not let go of what was wrenched from his bare hands. His stories converged in their source, after which each narrative went its own way. He never reconciled with Partition, and this aspect forms the basis of much of his fiction.

Asif Farrukhi
March 2020

It Is What It Is

(Jo Hai So Hai)

We are already sitting in the train.

Yes.

And we will reach the same destination as all its passengers.

Yes.

And these passengers have to reach where these rail tracks lead.

Yes.

But can we not go where these rail tracks don't reach?

Yes, can we not get there?

How can we get there?—Wait, there is one possible plan.

What?

That we get off the train.

Even if we got off, the train would still go where it is meant to.

Yes, but by getting off, we would remain here, where we are.

Yes, if we stay right here, then how will we reach where we are supposed to?

But where do we have to reach?

Where this train shall take us?

No.

Where else then?

There, where we wish to reach.

So get off the train and start walking to your destination.

But if we use our legs, when will we get there?

Now, or sometime, or never?

Now? How would we do that?

Maybe our destination is nearby.

And sometime?

Maybe the destination is a little far, or very far.

And never?

Maybe we will never reach there even if we keep walking.

So it is better that we stay seated in this train and reach wherever it is taking us.

This train will only take us on its tracks.

But we must reach where we have to reach.

And the train will go where it must.

Yes.

Then we should try to reach where we have to reach.

Come, then, let's get off the train.

No, stay, there are still three to four minutes before the train departs. Maybe we are meant to reach where the tracks lead.

The destination this train is headed towards has a name.

But we don't know the name of our destination.

And the train will reach its destination at the time it is meant to.

But we have no idea when we will reach the place we are supposed to reach.

It means that the train has to reach somewhere, and we have to reach some other place.

But if we sit in the train, then we will also reach where the train has to reach.

But we have to get elsewhere.

So, come—let's get off the train.

No, we have to reach where the train shall take us.

Where does the train have to reach?

That destination has a name.

But the destination we have to reach has no name.

So, come—let us get off the train.

But if we get off the train, where will we get to?

If we get off, we will be left right here.

Yes, we must not stay, we must go.

Where to?

There, where we must go.

Where to?

If we have to go, then we must get somewhere.

But where to?

Should I make it clear to you? Wherever we reach is our destination.

Then shall we continue sitting in the train?

No, we don't have to go anywhere.

Then come, let's get off the train.

No, even if we get off, where will we go?

We will go wherever we reach.

Then why did we come and sit in the train?

Because the train has to go somewhere.

But the train must go where its tracks lead.

And we, where our legs wish to take us.

Yes, but where to?

There, the train's whistle has blown.

Arrey, decide quickly!

Decide what?

Whether we get off or stay!

Yes—should we get off or stay?

Decide!

That is one thing I cannot do, decide.

Yes, we are without an identity only because of our indecisiveness.

Yes, and without a destination.

Yes, if I had the strength to decide, I would have fallen in love.

Would you really have loved?

Yes, and then I would have married.

What? Really?

And I would have had kids.

Really?

And my wife and I would have been seated comfortably in a room in our home and enjoyed the good fortune of listening to the sounds of our children playing in the next room.

Yes, there are such trains which have a full home in them.

Yes, and they also move on tracks.

Yes, they, too, go to the same place.

Then decide quickly if you wish to go or not.

No, I don't have the strength to decide.

But you will have to decide.

So, come, come, let us love.

Or—?

Or, should we not love?

Or—?

Or, should we fall in love and not fall in love?

That is what we are doing.

We should remain seated in the train and get off it as well.

Again, we are doing exactly that.

Yes, look there, outside the train—I am waving my handkerchief, saying farewell to myself.

Yes, truly, that is you.

Yes, I am leaving myself behind here.

Then get off the train.

No, I can't decide whether to get off or stay.

Decide, or you will be forever separated from yourself.

Yes, I know, once we leave a place, we cannot return there.

Decide quickly. The train is starting to move.

And if we return, we will find no clue of ourselves despite leaving no stone unturned.

There is still time to make your decision and get off. Otherwise, you will be forced to stay.

No, stay seated as you are. Look there—my eyes are filled with tears from waving and bidding myself farewell.

Yes.

Look—there I am, getting lost in the crowd—lost—getting lost.

Yes, the train has gathered speed.

I am lost!

Yes, we are still seated, and the train has started moving.

This is what happens when no one decides.

And what if they decide? What happens then?

Yes, oh yes, even then we get to be here.

If we had gotten off the train, it would have taken off and we would have remained right there.

Yes, just as now, when we didn't get off the train, and it is taking us away, and we are left behind there.

We meet ourselves only in the moment when we meet. And again the next moment. And again the following moment. And again the next moment.

But you are the one you meet.

Or the one who meets you?

The one I meet is myself. Then it is evident that it must be I.

Evidently...

And he who meets me is also I. Then it is evident that that must be I, too.

But who are you, really? He? Or Him?

I and Me!

And?

I and Me, and Me and I, and I...

But if I meet you, who do I meet?

Me—but I have been left behind, wrapped around the branch of that tree that covered its face with its flower-laden veil the moment I looked at it.

Yes, and the train moved ahead as usual on its tracks.

Yes, the train moves swiftly, and we can see what we see for fleeting moment. And after that moment, we keep seeing it in our mind.

Although it has been snatched away from our eyes.

Yes, but it seems as if it is with us.

Yes, but it is not with us.

Yes, nor are we with us—gradually, we too become a sight. Just a sight—nobody observing, but everything being seen.

Has a snake ensnared your eye with its stare?

Yes, I am that snake, turning to dust after biting myself.

And—?

And deposited in my place, I have turned into a mountain.

And—?

And I remain restless, eager to move from where I am. Look at that water rushing down the mountain—there! See?—at the change of the season, my own thoughts have started cascading from the peaks, running down the slopes.

If the season had not changed, would you have lain as snow on your own peak?

No, seasons would surely have changed; snow always melts, rivers always flow, water must play—

Yes, without water flowing down their slopes, mountains, too, resemble deserts.

But mountains are not deserts. Centuries of life—past and future—live within them. Dense forests, settlements, winding lanes, open roads, railway lines...

You describe them as if you have been there.

Yes, I have travelled the full distance within me from head to toe.

And from toe to head as well?

Yes, it is the same journey, whether from head to toe or toe to head.

But how did you escape your head?

Suddenly, while playing—

Yes, water must play.

Yes, and in its play, it flows down many slopes in myriad streams.

And it reaches where it is meant to as it flows.

Then come, let us get off the train.

Yes, let us scatter into many streams as we laugh and play.

But I cannot laugh and play.

Why not?

Because the train is moving so fast, my inner wholeness lies broken within me.

Yes, the feeling that I am just a moment, from beginning to end, is also being snatched away from me.

Yes, we have become moments.

There, look at the naked boy outside the window. He urinates facing us. And now that sturdy bull sways on all fours like a paddy field. And now that old donkey, perhaps once young—And now this—And now that—And this too—And that too—This—That—.

Yes, one by one, we have become moments.

Yes, and the train is so fast that each moment disappears from the eye before it has settled into it. This—That—This—That—.

Are you counting the seconds?

No, myself.

But if you count so fast, you will wrongly add up yourself.

So what? At least we will be added up.

What if someone checks?

No, who has the time to check us?

Yes, who is free to check us?

We have been added up wrongly.

Yes, and we are not what we have become after being added up wrongly.

And we won't go where these rail tracks lead.

But rail tracks will take us where they go.

Why worry about where this train is headed?

Yes, why worry? We won't go there.

Then let it go.

Yes, let it go.

But we are here, sitting.

No, I cannot see you.

Yes, I cannot see you either.

I don't know where we got off the train.
Yes, I don't know where.
And yet, here we sit.
Yes, we sit here.
And we don't have to go where the train goes.
Yes, we have to go somewhere else.
So it's good we got off somewhere on the route.
But we are still sitting here.
Yes, keep sitting. Everyone else is sitting too.
So do you have to go where everyone else is headed?
Yes—oh, yes! Everyone has to go there!

Dera Baba Nanak

(Dera Baba Nanak)

Some experiences break the barriers of the body and penetrate the soul, and after that, their grip persists for life. That is the reason why, throughout this half century, one dream has kept crawling into my sleep time and again. Right in front of me are cows and endless cows, and just behind them are dirty, chubby children, followed by old men with flapping snow-white beards. And finally, at the very end, there I am…

But why shouldn't I tell you the whole story?

At the time of the division of the nation, villages and towns were afflicted with such rioting that any young man who could escape and survive was considered brave-hearted. Hordes and hordes of people were coming from there to here and going from here to there. Finally, we managed to reach Dera Baba Nanak from Sialkot. When we had got on the train, we had no idea where we were headed. Across the border? Which border? What would the settled know about our journey? Which border did they ever have to cross, and to go where? But wherever our train halted, we dead people would gasp heavily for breath in the fear of having reached the threshold of the other world. As though, all at once, they would force their way into the train, raising loud slogans, and they would hack us, souls and all, into tiny pieces.

But we managed to cross the border. Here at Dera Baba Nanak, we saw that even before we had reached, we were lying here, scattered in every direction, and chopped into pieces—a hand here, a foot there, a portion of the liver, a well-rounded breast of some woman way over there, and here was a shrivelled male organ... withered and so tiny that it was impossible to tell whom it had belonged to—a Hindu, or a Muslim?

But, with us, a totally mad fellow had also arrived here. Nameless and fully crazy, nobody knew anything about him. Nobody knew where in Pakistan he had run away from to reach our refugee camp. Sometimes, the madman would start screaming, 'No, don't kill me. I am a Hindu—here, look! Look!' And he would lift his shirt and start untying the knot in his pajamas. 'Look at this!' And sometimes he would say, 'No, don't kill me. I am a Muslim—look at this...'

Suddenly, this madman saw the severed male organ lying in the dirt, and his hand reached into his pyjamas in sheer confusion and, probably finding nothing there, he impulsively ran to pick it up and stared with wide-open eyes at the severed penis, wondering if it belonged to him or someone else.

If there are thousands of reasons to cry, then, unconsciously, one starts to crave a little laughter. Several of us gathered around him, watching his state of mind playing out.

'No—it really is mine...' he tried to convince himself.

'How can it be yours, Madman? Only Muslims were cut into pieces here.'

'Achcha! Really?' The madman searched the severed organ for clues. 'Achcha!' It dawned upon him then that he must be a Muslim. Who knows what he was thinking when he clutched his own neck and pressed it with such ferocity that his eyes nearly popped out.

'You Musli…I will not let you get out of here alive, Muslim! Right in front of my eyes you killed my aged mother and father and raped my sister.' If somebody had not stepped in and made him let go, he would have taken his life with his own hands.

Just then, a strong rumour started spreading through the crowd that in a short while a kafila of Muslim refugees would pass by on foot to cross the border. That was enough to set things in motion. Everybody ran to their tents to bring sticks and spears to get ready for the plunder, grabbing the best positions beforehand, primed for action.

I heard the voice of a tilak-dhari from behind me. 'What progress will our nation make? This is the best opportunity to rid the world of these Malechha Muslims, not to simply loot their cash!'

'Oye, Pandit! Leave this noble task to us. We are here to do it. Come, friends!'

But just then, a loud voice bellowed from the loudspeaker outside the office of the refugee camp. 'Brothers, listen carefully! A small contingent of Muslims is crossing over to there, but a much larger contingent of Hindus and Sikhs is arriving from there. If our side creates any problem for them, they will not hesitate to spill the blood of our brethren. Beware, brothers! Do not attack them even by mistake. Watch from a distance and just let them go—beware!'

Disappointed, people started scattering around the wide road leading to the border on which the Muslim refugees were supposedly going to pass.

'Brothers, listen carefully! A small kafila of Muslims is crossing from here to there…'

I turned my attention away from the booming sound and looked at the madman, who still could not figure how his penis, dangling between his two legs, had suddenly disappeared. If only he could find it, he would satisfy himself whether he was a Hindu or a Muslim.

I sat right there on a small mound of earth and watched his antics.

It is not the echoes of the silence of emptiness that had made the madman go crazy but the surge of thoughts in his mind. As a result, he could not resist some notion taking hold of his mind, and he suddenly got up to collect scattered body parts, and started to put together a complete replica with them. He busied himself in this task for a long time, and I kept looking at him with fascination. With great effort, he would put together something resembling a human and, gazing at it, he would shake his head and change the order of body parts all over again to create another figure. He made several such shapes and each time got disappointed and scattered the parts. I suspected that a particular shape, which put him in great distress, was stuck in his mind and he wanted redemption by getting it out.

As I watched, he suddenly jumped and, with great fear, taking a few steps back, began staring at the new figure he had fashioned out of cut and damaged human parts. It was the shape of an ugly, ghostly monster that wanted to sink its teeth into the madman's body.

Terror-struck, the madman let out a shriek and started running. He ran in a straight line towards a remote corner of the road from where the dust cloud of the caravan of Muslim refugees moving towards the border could be seen.

I was happy that the madman had finally succeeded in getting the ghostly monster out of his mind. But he was still running. When he hid himself in a clump of trees ahead, I turned towards the side of the wide road close by. I walked towards it too. On both sides of the road, army men were deployed at short distances to ensure that the Muslim refugees cross to the other side safely. Crowds of Hindu and Sikh refugees began to swell behind every army man. Luckily, I got a good spot to stand and watch. I stopped and lit a cigarette, and the army man began to eye me suspiciously, asking me to step back.

I immediately stepped back and rested my back against a tree trunk and, while waiting for the kafila, I began to think of my mother. Rioters had attacked our house. With daggers drawn, they moved towards me, but my mother came in between and, writhing in agony at a swift cut of their sword, she lost her life instantly. The rioters did not even turn back to see who had died, my mother or me.

Standing in the courtyard of our home, I was gathering the wood stored for the kitchen to light my mother's pyre when two Sikh army men barged in.

'Get on! Leave!'

'But my mother?'

'Let those who have died be and save your life. Now move!'

The soldier standing guard near the road eyed me suspiciously again and this time, I moved back from the tree without him asking. Meanwhile, the front edge of the kafila drew near.

At the head were healthy white and brown cows, as the refugees knew that the Hindus would never attack cows. Behind the cows were exhausted-looking, chubby and dirt-smattered children. They knew that the Hindus think of children as manifestations of God, so, these little gods were heartlessly made to walk on their tired, swollen feet. After the children came weak old men, whose trembling white beards made sounds like birds flapping their wings. Every old man was supported by the young, as people would pity the old and, therefore, not attack the young. And behind them came wailing and lamenting old women and their caring, young daughters or daughters-in-law. How could anybody cast an evil eye on these dutiful daughters-in-law or their virginal sisters-in-law?

And following them all was a mixed group of middle-aged men and women with infants wailing in their arms or dangling over their shoulders, loud cries of Allah-u-Akbar ready to pour forth from every mouth the moment they crossed the border, as if a miracle had occurred…

And—oh! Behind everybody, even the last frail, tired mother carrying her infant on her shoulders… there was… our very own Madman!

'Look, brother!' Reeling with utter surprise, I tried to tell the army man that this mad person had come with us from the other side.

'Sh-sh!' The army man placed a finger on his lips and asked me to step back further.

I could not take my eyes off the madman. Is he a Muslim? No, he is of course a Hindu, but then, but then...

'*Look*, brother!'

'Sh-sh!'

Jungle

(Jungle)

Phantom Voice

Na, na, just lie there quietly, Jawan. There are thorns ahead. Several have pricked my palm. I can feel the bruises. I feel like aiming a gun at my palm to remove these thorns.

Inner Voice

This slow pricking feels life-threatening. What do you say, Jawan—isn't life just a thousand pin-pricks inflicted on us? They neither pierce us completely nor fade after pricking us, but just keep stabbing us, on and on, slowly. It would have been far better if the thorn had pierced right through to the other side of my palm, after which it could have been pulled out quickly—one minute of pain and after that, relief. Oh, but this continuous, slow stabbing!

Phantom Voice

Be gentle, bhai, you are shaking as if you are lying in your wife's lap, getting your white hair pulled out, not standing on a battlefield.

Inner Voice

Grey hair? Are you listening, Jawan? Ruthless life wears you out and makes you fight right through your years. You fight all your life, Jawan, and continuous fighting weakens all your faculties. Your hair begins to turn grey, you try to get rid of your grey hair but even more sprout, and... and then you become ice-cold.

Voiceless and Thoughtless

A mango bush to the left, a triangular cliff, two enemy soldiers, there could be more than two.

Phantom Voice

I have started to feel cold, Jawan. You, too?

Inner Voice

We have poured all the warmth and ammunition of our bodies into our guns. Why wouldn't we feel cold? Do our weapons, too, feel the enmity of our enemy?

Our weapons fight in obedience to our wishes, Jawan. And we fight in obedience to others. We, too, are weapons. *To the left, a mango bush, a triangular*... Bang! Bang! What enmity do I have with that man? Do I hate him for his identity? When we meet those we hate, we actually meet them with cordial smiles in our drawing room and assure them of our love—Bang! *I am so delighted to meet you*—Bang! *You did the right thing to come and meet us*—Bang! Bang! How happy we are to see them writhing under this shower of automated praise! How politely we force them to breathe their last. But this is our personal battle; we hate them so much that with great love and instinctive meanness, we decide to put them to death. Who was that enemy, hiding behind the triangular cliff? We never met each other; we neither love each other nor hate each other, but armed with rifles, we are embroiled in battle. We are automatic arms, like our automatic arms. Our wishes have no place in war or peace. Our duty is to strike peace without feeling and make war without feeling. Our soldiers are not courageous or cowardly—they are correct or incorrect. Correct soldiering is the name of battling without a conscience. Wipe out your enemy, wipe him out at all costs...

Thoughtless and Voiceless
The mango bush… the triangular cliff… two enemy soldiers… could be more than two…

Phantom Voice
Hey! Hey! Look, Jawan, something moves behind the triangular cliff. Ready? When this moving object shows itself, then… then… No—this thing is moving in my head! My eyes, focused on the outside, were too stunned to look inside my head.

Inner Voice
The sentry on duty suddenly went crazy last Sunday, and began showering bullets all around himself and into the emptiness, as if countless enemy troops were surging from his head at every moment and closing in on him in an unyielding circle. The madman, despite continuously spraying bullets, could not make even one of those fearful enemy faces fall, and eventually surrendered and lifted his arms and screamed, 'Spare me, spare me! What is my fault? I am a tool, whoever holds me by my hand, I am his tool. What else am I…?'

Phantom Voice

If this battle consumes you so, Jawan, then think—how many people will weep on hearing the news of your death?

Inner Voice

What will my wife be doing right now? She must be nursing Kitu, or teaching Vaman English. Vaman failed English in his last school examination. This time when I go home on leave, I will hire a private tutor for him. I want Vaman to be a doctor when he grows up, and when I am injured in a battle, I want to be operated upon by him. Last year, when our army doctor began to operate upon my leg, it felt as if he were opening a gun and cleaning it up, and that was it. Vaman is now in Class XI. One year plus two years plus five years… after eight years, my son will become a doctor and…

Phantom Voice

How many people will weep on hearing the news of your death, Jawan?

Inner Voice

On hearing the news of my death, Kitu and Vaman will struggle to weep given the depth of their pain, and poor Vaman will have to send everyone a telegram, but he doesn't even know enough English to write the message of his father's death. And he will suddenly start crying, and little Kitu will try to console him like an elder. The official telegram with the news of my death will lie in my wife's lap. It will grandly narrate my courage and indicate the amount of my pension, which the government will send in a few days. My wife will feel as if she is submerged in a dark well. I wanted to give her one more child: the first child hers, the second mine, and the third ours. And that child who belonged to us both was yet to be born but I would have died before his birth.

Thoughtless and Voiceless

Are we alive here, Jawan, or are we dead? Who knows? Who knows, we might have been waiting for the enemy and the enemy may have killed us and left. *The mango bush, the triangular cliff, two enemy soldiers, there may be more than two…*

Inner Voice

Those two soldiers speak my language. We have been taught different passions in the same language, which is what has divided us, made us from one into two. Two Punjabs. Two Bengals. Two Chinas. Two Vietnams.

Two Germanys. Two worlds. My mother is in the East and I am here in the West, and two armies stand, in the East and the West. And in the customs office, they are breaking the cake I had sent to my mother for her hundredth birthday into pieces and checking: could there be a timebomb in it? What if there really is? My aged mother, smiling and laughing, will lovingly eat the cake with the timebomb in it, and then that timebomb will reach her stomach and explode near her womb. And the geography of the East will disappear forever from my mind, the sun will never rise again; it will hang upside down between night and evening in the West, and its turgid rays, reddened with her blood, will haunt the entire world, and everyone driven mad by his own fear will attack the others.

Thoughtless and Voiceless
The mango bush...

Inner Voice
The mango bush is glaring at me. I am watching the bush back. Or is it that my eyes have fled from my face and plastered themselves on the face of the mango bush, from where they are now glaring back at me? Who knows, it may be that the ghost of some enemy

soldier I killed is lying in wait for me in the bush. Then, as I'm watching, the entire bush might uproot itself and start walking towards me and … and …

Phantom Voice

Be alert, Jawan. Are you looking at the mango bush? Look, it's shaking, shaking vigorously. You are silent, Jawan, lest you start laughing at my superstitiousness, but look—it is shaking from top to bottom, as if pulling out its roots to come at us. Beware, Jawan! I am going to start firing at it. Bang … bang … bang … bang … bang!

Inner Voice

I feel worn out after firing just one round. Continuously fighting in an army has reduced me to a coward and I want even my absentmindedness to be seen as bravery. But bravery? All brave soldiers know how cowardly they really are. In reality, baffled by their cowardice, they wish to be acknowledged as brave … bang … fear … bang! Hai! No, the silence has sent the sound of my firing slapping back into my ears. The silence has been absorbing those sounds ever since the beginning of creation, in which some may die or come alive. It immediately expels all other sounds from existence. This is the sound of the BANG.

Thoughtless and Voiceless

The mango bush... the triangular cliff... empty space... the raised spot ahead of the empty space... clumps of trees on the raised spot.

Phantom Voice

Pay special attention to this empty space, Jawan. If the enemies step out of here and into the trees, we might come within their range.

Thoughtless and Voiceless

Empty space... empty space... empty...

Inner Voice

This empty space appears as if it were full a moment ago, and many people had passed from here. Now, after being emptied out, it appears even more vacant. A little while ago, I think I saw someone crossing this path with extreme swiftness. Such silent swiftness—like the blink of an eye—or I am mistaken? No, I am not mistaken! Somebody has certainly passed from here. *Arrey*! *Arrey*! This little tree was over there some moments ago, about ten feet from the triangular cliff. How did it come near this empty spot?

Phantom Voice
Bang…Bang-bang-bang…Boom! Shot him, Jawan! He wanted to cross the empty spot in camouflage. *Arrey, arrey*! There is yet another one! Bang-bang… Boom. Oh! Look, Jawan, the tree has fallen from his hand and he is staggering and before he fell, he looked at me for just one moment.

Inner Voice
His dying look seemed to fade like a slide projected on a screen. In that brief gaze, I saw the entire city, decorated like a sacred festival. He sat in this jungle, but through his eyes, he was on holiday, enjoying the company of his wife and children.

~

'So, you are leaving by the evening train today?'

'It's only a matter of two or two-and-a-half months, darling, then I will return.'

'Kitu, Vaman, tell me what I should bring for you?'

'You yourself, Daddy.'

'I am sorry, Kitu and Vaman, I could not fulfil your innocent wish. Take care of your mother, Vaman…

'… don't let the children's hearts get polluted, darling.'

~

Just now, two suns appeared to shine on the forehead of my enemy, which lit up the whole world at once. But now, both the suns are shrouded in darkness. His dying gaze breathed its last on the lap of my gaze. At the very last moment, when no friend was around, he depended on an enemy... This one moment of friendship has brought back memories of all my previous births. In each birth, I forget my enemy, but I confront him in every birth. I die when he dies, and he is reborn with my life.

Phantom Voice
Come, Jawan, let us pray for the dead for a few moments. But beware! Not with eyes closed. And keep a strong vigil on my back and to my right. No enemy should suddenly attack me. I can take care of the front and left.

Empty space... a high spot... a clump of trees!

Phantom Voice
It's possible that there is no other enemy soldier apart from these two. Still, you must keep a special watch over the low trees.

Phantom Voice
Trees and humans are lying dead. A tree dies if it is pulled out of the soil, and if a human is buried in the

ground, that place becomes his grave. Trees, humans, humans, trees, tr…

Phantom Voice
Do you think trees are really alive like us, Jawan?

Inner Voice
Yes, they are alive like us animals, but their birth is different from ours. We take birth within ourselves and after that, we can go anywhere. At every place, we keep growing and blossoming, gaining selfhood within ourselves. But trees are born outside of their existence, sprouting from a seed in one place where they grow and blossom. They spend their entire life in that one place, where they gain very great heights.

Phantom Voice
Oh, if only we were trees!

Inner Voice
In an earlier time, earth must have had trees and only trees. We humans, too, might have been trees, and then many trees, all standing, must have had the desire to walk and move around. The intensity of this desire must have developed four legs on trees. Their life force buried in their roots must have come to inhabit their bodies, and then they must have scattered in the

jungles to run around on four legs. The more powerful among them would have survived by consuming the weaker ones. Then, some of those animals would have had the intense desire to walk on two legs, and they are the ones who became humans.

Phantom Voice

In the ancient stories, it is said that peepal trees could talk like humans. Yes, the peepal seed is the first human seed, and while becoming human, it came up out of the ground and could now roam the entire earth. He survives anywhere because he is above and not below the earth.

Thoughtless and Voiceless

Clumps of trees. Clumps of trees. Clumps of trees.

The earth is responsible for the survival of the trees because they surrendered their lives and their roots to it. However, humans took their lives in their own control, and can live anywhere in the world, and even outside it, in space—wherever they like. That is why they are responsible for their own freedom and existence. This responsibility means that they must develop a new capability in every new age. There is no alternative for them other than to evolve in every age.

Phantom Voice

Then answer my question, Jawan. Are human beings really evolving?

Thoughtless and Voiceless

Triangular Cliff. Empty space. (In the empty space, two humans, each within itself, and one tree, outside itself, lie dead.)

Inner Voice

We involuntarily wish that instead of our two legs, we could walk on all fours, and with the intensity of this desire, we become four-legged. Then, fed up of our animal lives, we would desire to surrender the responsibility for our survival to the earth, and become trees, and…

Phantom Voice

With the intensity of desire we will become trees and only trees and more trees will remain in the world.

Thoughtless and Voiceless

Clumps of trees, clumps of trees, clumps of trees…

Doves

(Fakhtayein)

'*Yahan khariyat hai, aapki khariyat neq matloob.*' (Everything is fine here, I hope you are well, too.)

While writing a letter to his old friend, Fazaldeen, Lobh Singh is reminded of the old days. Even then, Fazaldeen used to correct him for writing 'khariyat'.

'Lobhe, you are an Urdu teacher. And you don't even know that the word khairyat begins with khair.'

'Fazaldeen, don't behave like a theologian! Fewer the number of nukhtas in a letter, easier the writing becomes!'

'But…'

'Forget the ifs and buts; you too teach English.' They were both teachers in a primary school in Chawinda,

Punjabi Pakistan. 'Think again seriously. Why is this English language of yours so simple that even the Englishmen's kids can speak it fluently? Why don't our Punjabi kids speak Urdu with the same ease?'

'Lobhya, do you consider me your student? Why are you conversing with me in Urdu?'

'Because you are replying in Urdu! Haha.'

After the creation of Pakistan, Lobh Singh migrated to Delhi from his beloved Chawinda. He left his teaching profession and became a taxi driver.

'Friends, once you leave your home behind,' he used to say, 'you always seem to be on the run.'

After living in Delhi for a number of years, one day, all of a sudden, he received an envelope with a Pakistani postage stamp: 'From Maulvi Fazaldeen, Headmaster, Chawinda.' Reading the letter, he felt he was embracing his dear friend Fazaldeen tightly. 'Fazaliya, oh you bastard! You have become such a big maulvi and I had no clue about it! Oye! You big headmaster!' All five waters of Punjab streamed down his face into his beard.

'Has someone died, Father?' Jaswant Singh, his young son asked.

'No, my son, a corpse has come alive.'

After that, Lobh Singh made it a rule to leave all important work aside and sit down to write a letter to his Fazaldeen every month: '*Yahan khariyat hai. Aapki khariyat*?' (Everything is fine here. How are you?)

Lobh Singh started laughing uncontrollably whenever he remembered that even Fazaldeen's wife used to kick that dark-complexioned Maulvi out of his home.

'So, Fazaldeen, did you get beaten up today?'

'No, Lobhya, not today. Today is salary day!'

'Friend, my poor Dharam Kaur remains bedridden with fever even on salary days.' Lobh Singh's wife was always down with chronic fever.

'Come along today, I will take you to my uncle. He is a famous hakeem.'

'Fool, I am completely hale and hearty. It is your sister-in-law who is ill.'

But he wasn't well either. His wife's illness was eating him up inside.

During the intense violence and turmoil of the partition of the country in 1947, Lobh Singh and Dharam Kaur lost their home and so they migrated to Delhi in India. Had they still been living in Chawinda, Dharam Kaur would somehow have survived. They had not even completed one year of their stay in Delhi but in that chaos and commotion, Lobh Singh had to entrust his Dharam Kaur to Wahe Guru the Almighty.

'Sachche Padshah, my true God, until I complete my time here and return to you, please keep her safely in my account.'

'My time is already over,' Lobh Singh raised his head and asked himself, 'then what am I still doing here?' Stroking his white beard impatiently, he thinks he might begin his search for Wahe Guru, but where would he find Him? And in this long time, Dharam Kaur would have become old and weary like him.

But while she was dying, her face had become radiant because of her high fever. Holding her hand, he would sit by her on her bed as if, no matter what, he would stop her from leaving.

'Stop worrying, Jassi's father, I won't go away,' she used to say to raise his spirits, 'Don't be afraid. I won't go away. I know, if I die you will also die.'

This is what she said, but Dharam Kaur still passed away. And even worse, how long was Lobh Singh to continue breathing after her death? The whole world remained unchanged while he aimlessly drove around in his taxi. He kept eating as he ate before, and laughing and speaking too, but without his Dharam Kaur, he had become a living corpse. When Dharam Kaur was about to die, he held her hand tightly, but her hand remained in his while she migrated to an unknown destination.

Earlier, even if she went just to her natal home in Kotla Lohara, without fail, he would write her a letter every alternate day from Chawinda.

To,

Sardarni Dharam Kaur,

C/o Sardar Ranjit Singh (Ghodonwale),

Post office: Kotli Lohara,

Tehsil: Wazirabad,

District: Gujranwala.

But to which address should he send her a letter now? Right now, he is writing a letter to his Fazaldeen: '*Aapki khariyat neq matloob*.' (He can't stop cracking this joke!)

In any case, what use are courteous words between friends this close? When writing to Fazaldeen, Lobh Singh felt as if he sat in the fourth-standard classroom of his primary school.

Indeed, in Punjabi, you could show love even while scolding someone, but when you write a letter in Urdu, you must address the honourable addressee with courteous words such as 'aap'. This reminds him of people from Delhi who, even while abusing each other, use very polite words: *Aapki ma ki, aapki behen ki*… (Your mother's—! Your sister's—!)

He burst out laughing.

'What has happened to Father?' Leaving his wife, Jaswant Singh came running towards him.

Lobh Singh has been behaving strangely from the day he stopped driving. He would start laughing or crying for no apparent reason. Jaswant counselled his father to accompany the drivers on their trips, and told him that if he sat at home without work, he would go mad soon. As always, Lobh Singh replied, 'If you are so concerned about my well-being, then why don't you give me a grandson?'

'Father, you really have gone mad!' He asked his father, 'Are grandsons sold in some market? No man can go in a taxi and just buy one. One needs to put in some effort to have a baby.'

'Then make the effort, my son!'

In his daughter-in-law Pehlo's room, Jaswant's wife laughed in a mellow voice. Jaswant, too, smiled and returned to his room, shaking his head.

Lobh Singh was reminded of some letter from Fazaldeen in which he had mentioned that he has a total of fifteen grandsons and five granddaughters. It means that my daring headmaster has multiplied from one to twenty! Had he been living in this neighbourhood, I would have asked him for a couple of his grandchildren as soon as they were born. I would have bathed and cleaned them, combed their hair, and taken care of them—No, it's not possible that my Fazaldeen would deny me! I would have brought them here by force if he had refused, saying, 'If they are yours, does it not mean they are also mine, Fazaldeen? Read your holy book carefully, headmaster! There are clear instructions that you should share with all friends and buddies.' Kadah Prasaad, our sacred food offering, is for all the Sangat; for everybody to eat together, but may his Allah keep him happy and my Wahe Guru keep me happy. Why would Fazaldeen not listen to me?

Persuaded by his greed and ambition, Lobh Singh has driven his taxi to the door of Fazaldeen's house and woken up all his friend's grandsons and granddaughters with his honking. He has gathered all the children, stuffed them in the car, and brought them to Delhi. 'Behold the grandeur of Qutub Saheb! And there—that is his Lordship's office—this Lal Qila!

Yes, brother, give one-one kulfi to each kid. Enjoy your kulfi, children! The kulfis here are qulfis with the Qaf, as in qainchi. They have the power to clear a congested throat. Hahaha. O Shabbo, why are you going that way? Come here. We will walk to Chandni Chowk from here, come!—Be careful!—careful! Sitting right there, Lobh Singh is exhausted after taking the children around and, breathless with joy, he is now back in his own room.

'*Yahan khariyat hai.*' (All is well here.)

'*Haan khariyat hai. Khariyat toh hai.*' (Yes, all is well. Well it is.)

Khee, khee, khee, ha ha!

From the next room he heard his son and daughter-in-law's muffled laughter and asked himself with resignation, 'What else is it to be well? Even on that day seven-eight years ago, when everything had shattered, I had given Fazaldeen news of being well. It had not even been a month since my elder son, Jaswinder Singh, had left for his heavenly abode in that car accident. I was left displaced once again, and this time, even my mind and soul could not shelter me.

But if I can't be a source of happiness for my distant friend, then why should I be a source of his sorrow? If there is no other option but to become a source of sadness, then the basket of sorrows should be opened slowly, so that only the tail end of the black serpent is visible at first.

'Is Jaswinder Singh the name of your son?'

'Yes. Why?'

'Did he take a taxi to Agra yesterday?'

'Why, what has happened?'

'Yesterday! Yesterday, his taxi hit a motorcycle. The rider died on the spot.'

'My son is innocent! He is a responsible driver, sir.'

'Yes, but at the same time, a speeding truck came upon his taxi from behind and...'

The black serpent spread its hood now—but Lobh Singh has already mustered up all his courage.

Just about a week after the accident, Jaswinder Singh was supposed to get married, and Lobh Singh had extended invitations to every member of the local taxi drivers' union. The Commissioner of Transport had stood up from his chair and shaken hands with Lobh Singh, promising his presence at the wedding. This was to be the first wedding in his family and he had planned a celebration with much pomp and show. And although he had sworn not to drink alcohol again, he would drink a couple of sips that day. Wahe Guru is our own guy and he knows that it is only human to commit small mistakes on such big occasions! Otherwise, what is the point of living! I will ask him to sit beside me and drink. 'Take this, my brother, today you should also taste a few drops. No?...No, my Sacche Padshah, just take a couple of sips, for my sake!'

Lobh Singh can hear the sounds of music and celebration. Just behind the musical band, he sees Jaswinder in all his finery, riding a horse. He is wearing a scented golden rose-and-pearl sehra over his turban. A little ahead, wearing salwar-kameez and crowned with a wavy, striped, saffron turban, Lobh Singh himself walked, as if going to perform a bhangra. Every now and again, he turns around to sprinkle kewra-scented water on the marriage procession. The faces of the people in the entourage are radiant and their laughter bursts like crackers.

And, and, now what is this? The whole marriage procession has suddenly started floating above the ground! They are ascending towards the moon and the stars while singing and dancing. Only Lobh Singh and his younger son, Jaswant, have remained on the ground and are shouting madly: 'Veer-ji...'

'Jaswinder...'

'Wait, son...'

And then, feeling helpless, he rubs his hand. His turban has loosened and fallen on his shoulders. He tells a passersby, 'He is such a good son, exceptionally good. He went up to take the blessings of his dead mother.'

Lobh Singh cries softly.

'What has happened, Father?' This time Jaswant asks from his room.

'Nothing,' Lobh Singh says, as he wets his towel and cleans his face and then comes and sits on his bed.

'*Yahan khariyat hai*...' (All is well here.)

'*Kahan khariyat hai*?' (How is it well?)

But Wahe Guru's will must be accepted in good spirits. 'Everything is fine, son,' he says loudly to save his son from worry, 'Relax.'

He took the letter in his hand and started writing again:

'The situation here is that it is difficult to pass the time. Day and night, I lie quietly in my bed. The only worthwhile moments are when I doze off and reach my Chawinda.'

Lobh Singh then heard his mother's voice from fifty-five or sixty years ago, 'Lobhya, Lobhya.'

The elderly Lobh Singh answers unthinkingly in the voice of the same young Bebe da Lobhya. 'Yes, Bebe.'

'Go, son, Fazla is at the door calling for you,' Bebe's voice said.

What a life it was! Life handled all its responsibilities itself. Our task was just to grow up while enjoying it.

Lobh Singh takes a deep breath and starts writing again:

'Is it not possible for you to fill your pockets with the soil of Chawinda and come to meet me? You can cross the border secretly if you don't get a visa. What have we to do with the battles between the powerful? We inconsequential people meet just for the sake of embracing each other. Why should anyone have a problem with that? Come here secretly, and my son Jaswant Singh will take care of all the rest.'

Lobh Singh smiles as he hears his son and daughter-in-law softly giggling, and starts playing with his squealing grandson. 'Oh, Bhai Kesar Singh, oh

Gulab Singh, oh your mom's Motbar Singh,' and his mom's Motbar Singh kept squealing back in response. But where is he?

Disheartened, Lobh Singh held the letter in his hand again:

'The rest of my story is that I feel quite lonely here. A few months ago, when I completed my sixty-fifth year, Jaswant Singh asked me not to drive the taxi anymore and stay home. At first I wanted to slap him and tell him that my taxi is mine, I am mine—so who was he to interfere? But the truth is that now I don't have it in me to drive. Now I can only ride imaginary horses. If—*he scratched out the familiar mode of address 'tumhari' on the letter and wrote the honorific 'aapki'*—like you, I were in the headmaster position, I would have declared my age as younger and spent ten or fifteen more years on the job. But I have had enough of it. You enjoy the benefits of your pension and start teaching the children at home. If you continue teaching children outside your home even after retiring and getting your pension, then you will have to be sent to a mental asylum in a couple of months. Ha-ha-ha-ha.' Lobh Singh put down his pen.

Once, a cheerful elderly madman sat in his taxi and ordered him authoritatively, 'Drive.'

'Where to?'

'Back.'

Lobh Singh could not suppress his laughter, 'But the taxi can only move forward.'

'But I have to go behind myself.'

'Then, dear sir, what is the need to take a taxi? For that you should descend step by step into your own mind.'

Today, it is as if Lobh Singh has come to sit in his own taxi:

'Where to?'

'Chawinde.'

'Chawinde?' He takes himself for a madman and starts laughing.

'There is just one way to get there: through the skies. So, become a dove and fly there, Sardaro.'

'Why?'

Why?

Varyaam Singh was Dharam Kaur's brother and Lobh Singh and he used to be good friends. Varyaam Singh used to ask him: 'We migrated from Chawinda after everything was snatched away from us. Why do you want to return there?'

'Because Chawinda is my refuge, brother.'

Whenever the memory of Chawinda became too much for him to bear, Lobh Singh put everything aside and visited Varyaam Singh in Saharanpur, where he had settled after migrating from Pakistan. As soon as Varyaam saw him, he would ask, 'Have you come here to reach Chawinda?'

And Lobh Singh would reply, 'Open the bottle. We can talk later, when we reach Chawinda.'

Whenever Lobh Singh was unable to visit Varyaam Singh, he would sit down to write him a very long letter. 'Bhai Varyaam Singh, Sat Sri Akal, Everything is fine here. How have you been? The conditions are such that we have to reach Chawinda soon. So, uncork the bottle quickly.'

Even now, Lobh Singh often gets restless to write a letter to brother Varyaam Singh. But to what address should one send a letter for someone who is dead? Had he been alive, Lobh Singh would simply have walked to the door of the fourth house to the right of Koocha Dilbara, Saharanpur, to deliver his letter. But nobody knows the addresses Wahe Guru allocates to dead people. Even so, lost in his own flow, he once wrote a letter to his deceased brother-in-law, which was returned to him. Or, perhaps, it had reached the right address: when we communicate with a dead person, we have to reply to ourselves on their behalf, too. The one who had to die has died, but we are here to live his life.

Lobh Singh is dozing off, and as he dozes he roams about in his dreams, and as he wanders around he loses his way, and while still within his dream he emerges out of his dream—here—this is the Primary School, Chawinda. The dirt road before the school leads straight to his home. There—Dharam Kaur waits for him at the front door of his house. She stands there every day, waiting for him, even during her illness. He stops to look at her to his heart's content. He feels his woman has turned into gold and scattered everywhere like yellow mustard blossoms. He jumps all at once while staring at her: I, Lobh Singh, am staring at her while she burns with a high fever! He runs towards her, but no sooner does he cover half the distance, he finds her collapsing to the floor, smiling.

'Dharmo!—Jaswant—Jassi!'

'What's the matter, Father?' Jaswant has come running from his room.

'Nothing,' Lobh Singh tames the turmoil within himself.

'Go to sleep, Father,' Jaswant tells his father, and looking around the room, spots his unfinished letter. 'Are you writing a letter?' he casually enquires.

'Yes, to your uncle in Chawinda,' Lobh Singh replies after wiping his face with a towel.

'You have gone mad, Father.' Jaswant pities his father and reminds him that it is ages since the uncle in Chawinda has been dead and gone.

The Abyss

(Pataal)

Where am I?

In Europe, America, or Africa? Or on the Indian subcontinent?

I do not know.

I would be shot dead if I tried to go out to see where I am. Outside, there is a curfew.

The world around me is so silent that one feels like letting noise burst forth uninhibited. I am scared of noise, and yet my heart yearns for clamour.

Doomsday stood at the door earlier. Fire and blood, blood and fire. Helpless screams leapt from the mouth, as if committing suicide to save their lives.

'No, son, don't open the door.'

There is death everywhere outside, life has come running indoors, and the graveyard is full.

We must change how we interact with each other. Why must we insist on going out to meet each other? Rather than get impatient to embrace someone, we must convince ourselves that meetings happen only in our hearts. But how can we reach out to those in the graves next to ours? Well, those who live in graves can only be met in our mind.

'Bhaiyya, I am happy in my home. My husband is very nice, and so are all my in-laws. I am very happy, but when I remember you, Bhaiyya, my tears flow ceaselessly.'

'Arrey, silly girl, I am not far away from you. Here is Hindustan, and there, right next to it, is Pakistan. Just close your eyes for a bit and I'd be standing before you. No, don't cry. Am I a fool like you? My tears are also flowing.'

(Ya Allah, do souls cry?)

'Abba jaan, I want to go out.'

'There is a curfew outside, son.'

'Curfew must be lonely, Abba, please go out, save him. Else, people will kill him. Go, Abba, go! Bring Curfew inside.'

I had felt as if Curfew stood terrified outside our door. Secretly, I had got up to open the door, and when I tried to look outside, it had entered. Seeing its frightened face, I had run in terror to my room, where I entered my own being. An incident from two years ago had started flashing in my mind—a devil of a man, a heavy axe raised above his head, went thwack! and my elder son lay fallen. My strongest branch was chopped down, and white blood flowed from my trunk. I couldn't even cry out. My son's murderer wept then, saying his Ramu, too, was killed that way. He cried as if he had not killed my Rehmu. Unable to bear the grief of his son's killing, he had gone mad. He picked up my Rehmu with both his hands and lifted him above his head, and I extended my hands to stop him. But the hands of imagination do not have the power to grip anything. My son was murdered again.

~

I am the father of Robert F. Kennedy.

Joseph P.—you died in the Second World War. How come you have lined up for the Third World War, son? And John F., what did you whisper in Robert's ear that he, too, followed you?

You travellers to the afterlife, understand that no one ever finds anyone there. Instead of wandering the sands of this faceless universe, stay right here. If you live, you can meet in your imagination even if you are separated. But once you die, your imagination, too, dies with your body.

Come here, Edward M., you dying flame in the lamp of the Kennedy family. Come and sit with your old father. Let us have coffee, son, and talk of the good old days when God almighty bestowed us with eternal grace.

No, son, don't blame Jesus's father for these bad days. God is merciful under all conditions. If he weren't, you would have died like your brothers.

Arrey, where are you going, Edward, my child? Do you feel stifled in these graves? I, too, suffocate here, son. But the graves are safe. Corpses never die. Nobody will kill you here. Won't you stay? Why not? You too, son…?

~

'Are you going to the door again, son? Beware, Curfew is outside.'

'Abba, I will play outside with Curfew.'

How do I explain to my innocent child that those other people had also come to play with Curfew?

And what a merry game it was! A game of lights so enchanting that they deceived the eye. Humans burned, and it looked as if fireworks had been set off. Why deny it? It's not every day that the opportunity to play with fireworks shows up. So give a big hand, applaud, and have a good laugh—if people scream, it will seem as if the fireworks are cracking up with laughter. Buildings will appear to topple over from being tickled, and then roll on the floor mirthfully. Laugh, keep laughing, so that you no longer remember when one should laugh, or make others laugh. Is there ever a fixed time to laugh? One laughs when one feels like it!

An American asked an Englishman: 'Why does your face strain so when you laugh?'

'Because we force ourselves to laugh at appointed times to exercise our faces.'

'This habit destroyed your empire, whereas we laugh for no reason and force everyone around us, too.'

'And if they don't laugh for no reason?'

'Then we shoot them dead.'

'Martin Luther King! Did you hear that? You were shot dead because you refused to laugh when there was no reason to laugh. I agree, you had no reason to laugh.

Wait—doesn't saving a life count as a good enough reason to laugh? But then, perhaps your life would have remained in danger even if you had laughed. If white people could not see sadness flicker on your darkled face, how would they have found a hint of your happiness in *this* darkness? You had to be killed under any circumstance, Martin Luther King, because the darkness on your face creates suspicion, and American civilisation is terrified of the dark. That is why it wishes to always be illuminated. It wants education for light, it longs for light, kills for light. From fear, American civilisation even sleeps in the dazzling bright light. So why wouldn't the unblemished shadows of the Black face upset them? Darkness recedes when light grows. Darkness must end—let it end. You Black people are needlessly rioting. These riots, this Curfew, this assault of artificial light, this restless darkness will go extinct in the circle of brightness. Let there be light—more light!'

'Abba, I will go out!'

My son does not know that outside, boundless light will grasp his being from all sides. It will take him in its clutches, constrict him, and pierce his body. He will no longer be visible in that boundless light. A blinding light akin to darkness, a totally empty light, will take his place.

Instead of going out, I wish to enter the dark subterranean layers of the earth with my son. Crawling through these layers will graze our hands and legs. Our heads and torsos will be smoothened, our edges will be rounded. Our limbs will slowly disappear. We will turn into a new species of snake. Snakes have long lives because of their subterranean existence. The steady darkness of such an existence lengthens life. Instead of dying of the poison in the earth, snakes collect it in their hood, where it thickens and coalesces, solidifying to become the snake's gemstone that illuminates darkness.

My son was baffled, or I would have told him, 'Come, son, let's get buried in the earth.' He suddenly started to sob uncontrollably.

'Don't cry, son, don't cry—quiet! Quiet, be quiet now!'

Remembering his deceased mother, whose face he has forgotten, has made my son cry. Or, perhaps, it was not being able to remember his mother's face that made him cry. I, too, cannot remember my mother's face. We are all orphans, unable to find our reflection in any other's face, as if no one is our own. 'Come, son, come to me.'

My son is quiet now. Perhaps feeling the weight of my hand on his delicate shoulder has made him anxious; he thinks I may beat him if he makes a noise. He will grow into his youth, eying me with suspicion, the root of his hatred for me growing and spreading within him. Perhaps he will take care of me when he grows up because he hates me…We are all orphans, and we have forgotten those we acquired our primal faces from, so we find all faces alien, and we see a familiar stranger in everybody we meet. Indeed, we have no one and, since we are familiar only with strangers, we lie when we tell people they are ours.

'Come here, son!' My son has not gone silent because of his own volition but because of overwhelming fear. Silent in his confused state, he may feel that I will strangle him.

After all, Rehmu was also killed by a father!

'Don't be scared, my prince! Why are you scared? I will take you to see the whole town tomorrow, once the curfew is lifted. There is nothing to be scared of, everything will be okay by tomorrow, dear son.'

By tomorrow! We been saying forever that

everything will be okay by tomorrow. Has our world turned upside down? Have we tumbled off our satellite into the void? All time is present here. Tomorrow never comes.

'Son, till tomorrow...'

Shut up! It's not like you will reach the moon tomorrow. Your rocket has sunk in the void. Every molecule of your globe has drowned in the void and become a part of the void. Son, can you hear me? Am I really speaking? Or am I just imagining that I am talking? Do I exist? Do you exist? Don't even souls dissolve in space?

'Should I tell you a story, son? It is a really fun story, will you hear it?' I don't know which story, but I'll tell one that will bring joy to my child's heart, drive away his fear, make him want to burst into laughter. I'll tell a cheerful story of a virtuous man's bright future.

(Shut up, don't lie!)

'Once there was...' I begin.

'Once there was...' But who was? I scratch my head, wondering.

'Once there was a very virtuous man.' Very virtuous indeed! Who was this good man? Tell me his name, address, and profession. And prove that he was truly virtuous. Tell! Tell! *He was a very good man*. So present the proof of his goodness.

'That man ...' My fearful son laughs at my confusion. And my heart felt so light that I forgot to continue with my story.

'Abba, why do we remain inside the house whenever Curfew is outside?'

Little does my innocent son know—if no curfew is imposed outside, there is one imposed within. Like when the world bustled outside, but guards were stationed at Pasternak's door. Each heart sings its own song, nor does a consensus exist in thought; but Pasternak's unspoken ideas would have exploded in his brain if he didn't write them down. Still the guards told him, 'Let your brain explode, or a bullet will be shot into it.' And Pasternak responded, '*Arrey bhai*, at least read what I have written.'

'No, baba, we don't understand your tongue—nobody who speaks my language does.'

'Well, even so, I must speak. *Here*—I am speaking right now. This is the moment of my liberation. Stop me, and poison will spread through my veins, killing me along with my unborn words. O Europe, O America, O Asia, or Africa, those who speak my language refuse to listen to me, but I am still speaking. You don't understand my language, but listen to me! The same tongue lives in all our mouths—heed my call.'

Curfew!

'Abba, you will take me out tomorrow, na?'

'Yes, son, yes. I will definitely take you out.'

But tomorrow, too, Curfew will be around, and the day after tomorrow. Everyday! How will I fulfill this wish of my son? I look at his hopeful face.

'I will surely take you, son.'

I feel I am not in my home, but that I lie alone in this room in my body, and my son is beating on its doors. From fear of Curfew, I dare not open the latch.

Free Spirit

(Khulabaaz)

I don't understand why people are surprised when they learn that I am a fantasist. Let alone the general public, even aviation experts are momentarily taken aback when they see me in a pilot's uniform. Even during the interview for the selection process, I was asked why, despite being a woman, I prefer this profession.

'Despite being a woman?' I could not help smiling, though I was somewhat nervous owing to the interview.

'Yes, yes, go on, tell us why you want to become a pilot.'

'Because it is the inherent nature of woman to incessantly fly in the air.'

The chair of the interview board burst out laughing.

Hearing his guffaw, other members of the board became extraordinarily serious, so serious that it aroused more laughter.

'You are right! We men, even while soaring through the sky, feel as if we are walking on the ground, but you women, even when you are standing near your kitchen counters, seem to be aboard a Boeing 707.'

'Yes, sir,' I replied inadvertently and became flustered at my response.

'Why did you not apply for the job of an air hostess?'

'I don't like being the host or the guest!'

A flustered person, when riled further, ends up speaking their mind.

'Here is what I desire. I want to feel at home in whichever country I visit, like any person in that country.'

'Arrrr ... ' The chair of the interview panel burst out laughing again.

~

Anyway, I was selected and I have been flying in the sky regularly for many years. London, New York, Moscow, Rome, each destination is familiar to me like my own place. I find them as familiar as one can be with the strangeness of one's in-law's house.

I have a very special sweet friend at every location. So sweet that whenever I encounter him, I feel as if the earth is swirling around. Last week, as I was suffering from a bit of a cold, I could not reach London on my assigned day. But now, as I arrive here on my latest visit, Aftab is waiting patiently for me as usual.

'You have arrived! Come,' he says and we sip our morning tea together as always.

'You must have had your breakfast alone the last time I was expected?'

'No, you were here with me.'

I know that Aftab is not creating a fiction about my presence: a young and healthy existence is not filled with the ugliness of cunning. A heart brimming with young blood keeps on beating without a thought; it does not reflect or think before every heartbeat.

Aftab is very naive and I constantly fear that the rather indifferent and fast-paced London will suddenly, unknowingly, crush my friend under its pressure one day, and no one will even know it has happened. Then, when I will visit London on a scheduled trip, someone else will be occupying Aftab's rented room.

The world is so crowded that if someone passes away, somebody else spontaneously occupies the place they have vacated. The universe never accepts a vacuum; it keeps changing.

'I am really sorry, Madam,' some strange old Englishman will look out from Aftab's window and inform me, 'Aftab Husain is not here.'

'Where is he? Has he returned to Pakistan?'

'No, he left for his heavenly abode. He met with an accident.'

~

Why did you come here from Pakistan, Aftab?

When we first met, he was drinking with the seriousness of an old man in the lounge of the Young Life Club, as if he was performing some important obligation with great thought and sincerity. Several couples were on the dance floor, shaking their legs to the loud and rapid beat of the orchestra. Aftab's intoxicated eyes were riveted to their joyful, swaying bodies before him.

I came and sat near him, hoping that he would become comfortable with me within a couple of minutes, and then, in typical Eastern style, request me to dance with him. Then, soaked with all the familiarity of dancing together, we'd get exhausted and go to a restaurant for dinner as usual and after that he would say, 'Come, let me take you to my place. Will you come?'

Instead, after becoming friendly with me, tears started flowing from his eyes and I panicked and started looking around. After a while, in a sad, drunken voice, he started talking about his old mother who lives alone in some village in Pakistan and to whom he sends ten pounds from his salary on the very first day of each month. Then, all of a sudden, he took my hand in his own and, swearing by his mother, confessed that he had really and truly fallen in love with me.

'Why did you come here from Pakistan?'

'Because I had to meet you. One has to reach Amritsar from Lahore via London.'

Aftab is Pakistani and I am an Indian, an Indian who, before the creation of Pakistan, was a native of that part of India which later became a part of Pakistan.

My first love affair was with a very naive boy. What a sweet, innocent, and childish romance it was, when the only wish from the beloved is that they reciprocate your love. Indeed, it is a great feeling. In India and

Pakistan, many boys' beloveds and many girls' lovers have migrated across the borders of both countries. And since they are unaware of the route to London, they feel as if their beloved has left them for good—for their heavenly abode—and that they will never meet again. Now, when one lover remembers the other, their mind echoes with the explosion of bombs. But here in London, my hand held by Aftab's hand, I feel as if the old India-Pak subcontinent has drowned and an ocean has reclaimed its territories. All London's ills have been washed away in the germ-purifying waters of this ocean and the subcontinent has blossomed in delight all over again.

Aftab's presence has never aroused any wicked thought in my mind. Whenever I see him, pure maternal feelings awaken in me and I feel my body burst into light. This is what saves Aftab's boat from being wrecked on the rocks in turbulent waters.

'I will shoot your Pakistani friend,' said a young Englishman dancing with me at the annual London Air Club dinner.

'Why?'

'Why not? Are you not yet bored of each other's company?'

'No.'

'Quite strange!'

I smiled.

'That Pakistani guy should realise that I am also in the queue. Even the longest queues are cleared in minutes in our London.' I smiled some more.

'This isn't funny, Miss Madhu. He has been in the way for many months. Is it proper?'

I don't fully understand what category of relationship I have with Aftab. When I hug him, my desires are satiated and I feel a great sense of peace. He is more enamoured of my chastity than me. He has fallen for what he perceives is my virgin love. The poor fellow has no clue that I have a boyfriend in every city with an airport.

His blind faith is very dear to me. I think God, too, loves his innocent and naive believers.

In New York, I have an intense relationship with Vicky. The illegitimacy of that relationship is as acceptable as the legitimacy of my relationship with Aftab. On reaching London, my soul finds a satisfaction comparable to what my body experiences on arriving in New York. Here in New York, it feels as if my overworked, exhausted body has died and I have renewed myself all over again. If I do not bathe regularly in the soothing, clear waters of the American rivers, perhaps I would not muster the courage to retain my purity in London. The sins I commit here make me worthy of devotion there.

'Vicky,' I say, 'your wickedness gives me the courage to be virtuous.'

I often tell Vicky about Aftab but I never mention Vicky to Aftab. Perhaps, among wicked people, frankness grows naturally and flourishes like a lotus blooms in the muck. Good people remain lost in thoughts about looming dark clouds even on sunny days. But if dark clouds appear in the clear skies of the mind of an aimless wanderer, wouldn't it simply start to rain? In the same way, the virtuous are seen as liars even when they speak the truth. That is why I am truthful around Vicky and lie when I am with Aftab.

'May Allah protect me from infidels,' says Aftab the devout Muslim, 'If I were not a Muslim, I would have accepted you as my God.' His innocence naturally transforms me into a divine damsel, and the same divine damsel transforms into a princess in New York, where that playful Satan, Vicky, becomes my God.

Well, regressive society is right in teaching woman

to see man as her God. She cannot but worship the one she surrenders her body to. I, too, worship that naughty chap! I worship him impatiently and my restlessness ends in satisfaction. I don't know what came over me one day, but while prostrating before Vicky, I performed an arti instead. Vicky liked this sport very much and laughingly said, 'You have turned me into your omnipotent, dark-complexioned God. I have started to feel that the entire world survives due to me. I am God—I myself am God.'

Initially, I laughed, but then I looked at him and shrank back, 'Yes, it is true. You are God yourself.' He was the exact likeness of God. Vicky dominates my universe and me. If he were not around, I'd be unaware of myself. He knows all my sins and yet he has accepted my sinning self. He is my God who lives in my every breath. He is omnipresent for me; even in Moscow, where I flirt with Sholo; in Rome, where I find Faniska waiting for my flight to arrive in an exceptionally expensive suit—Faniska, who forgets all about the traffic rules while driving me to the hotel in his car. 'When you are close, I can think of nothing but you,' he tells me.

Whenever I tell Vicky about Faniska, my naughty

God gets slightly irritated. He looks so good when he is distressed that I give him plenty of brandy and drink a lot of it, too, and then, all of them appear, wearing different expressions—Faniska, Vicky, Sholo, Rami, Rowdy, Kawal, even Aftab. They are all dear to me; the bad appear good, the sly seem naive. And Aftab's soul enters their bodies, which dominate his soul. Their bodies dance; goodness and wickedness dancing to the same tune, tirelessly, exhaustingly, losing their individuality.

The dance is underway, fast and soundless, and I dance, too, perhaps in a vacuum, for my body feels weightless, as after a long swim.

I won't tire even if I dance like this for the rest of my life. I don't need anyone, neither the moon nor the earth, for my destination is this vacuum, the true home of a woman. If she reaches a stratum holding air, it will only weigh her down.

~

'Mummy, Mummy, Mum…' Knock-knock. I ran towards the door. I was in Room No. 5 of my working women's hostel, smoking one cigarette after the other while waiting for the postman.

Knock. I quickly unlocked the door, took the letter from the postman, and opened it right away.

'We are sorry. You have not been selected for pilot training.'

'Huh!'

It was as if I had suddenly become old and angrily plunked a plate of fried potatoes before my bald and chubby husband.

Janab-e-Aali

(Janab-e-Aali)

The home departments of Hindustan and Pakistan received two ridiculously long, rambling applications simultaneously (or not long after each other) from two applicants with the same name: Mohammed Mustafa.

Your applicant is a respectable middle-aged resident of his country and is professionally associated with higher education in the humanist tradition of classical Urdu literature.

At my age, a man starts paying attention to overcoming his day-to-day, routine problems so that, attaching himself to his God, he can spend his remaining life peacefully. But as destiny would have it, in my case, despite my prudence and innocence, the local police and intelligence units have troubled me no end with their irrelevant daily interrogations. When I approached my lawyer about it, in a four-line reply referring to human rights in our Constitution, he warned the government to take immediate steps to control the illegal activities of the officers. And then he explained to me at length that the government does not read long applications: 'If you want the government to read your application, then write your problem in the very first line and in the second, suggest a suitable solution for the problem yourself, and insist in a threatening tone that if necessary steps are not taken to address your complaint, you would have to fight for your legal rights.'

Still, my problem is that if I do not narrate my entire story, I choke and feel suffocated. The only problem with the desire to narrate a complete account is catching hold of where it began. Nonetheless, let me first tell you what my complaint is about. For the last many weeks, the shadows of your men have followed me in such a manner that I feel I am under arrest. It has reached the point where their shadows might knock on my mind very soon. There was only one way of escape, so I gathered myself and pondered over my condition, and decided that I should go to the police station and confess the sins I have not committed. *Which sins*? Yes, Janab-e-Aali, the ones which do not exist even in my subconscious mind. *But what is it that is not there in my subconscious mind*? One who teaches the loss of love and romance in classical Urdu literature, a harmless bag of bones, is taken to be a dangerous spy of the government across the border on the verge of destroying the very structure of our country, a country whose good performance has a direct relation to his own good life and that of his wife and children. *So*? So write whatever comes to your mind and get my signature on it, and—and have me hanged—what else?

No, no, Janab-e-Aali, I am only presenting, very honestly, a mirror to my present state of mind. Around two months ago, an officer of your intelligence service descended on my university campus to ask me some important questions. As I was entering my chamber, while gushing over my lecture on the simplicity and truthfulness of Mir's[1] language and expression, the gentleman asked me to sit—so curtly that it seemed as if I had come to his police station on his summons.

'These days, a lot of people are coming to your house from there,' he interrogated me immediately.

'From where?'

'From there! Where else from?'

I understood. Last month, my grandmother had come from across the border. (*'You have turned out to be exactly like your father. Just do your arithmetic, Mustafa, how many years have passed since your father died?'*)

I had not even counted the years when the inspector threw another question at me.

'Who was that moustachioed man with the old lady? What business did you have when you took him to the graveyard in the darkness of the evening?'

'Oh! My nephew? He wanted to offer fateha[2] at my father's grave.'

'Our information is that he was a very special man from their CID.'

'No, no. He is presently doing his MA in Urdu. He had come to take care of my ageing grandmother.'

'But in those very days, three men were killed in a bomb blast in Chhote Bazaar. Do you recall?'

I was taken aback and began praying for the dead.

'And tell me more,' he cut short my prayer, 'why had you gone to their embassy last Wednesday?'

Janab-e-Aali, why should your foot-soldiers descend

to threaten a person with imprisonment when he is himself bound by the Constitution? What do I have to do with an embassy? I have only been running around for a visa. My youngest sister is getting married there in two months. My little sister, whose hair has turned grey waiting for me, has written to me: 'I will stop my nikah if you do not come, my brother.' She was so tiny when my father died. My mother was not in her senses; I fed her and played with her, and any demand of hers would make my heart melt. I find it impossible to ignore her demands.

Are the human rights written into our Constitution meaningless or meant for real-life situations? Are we to lead a prescribed life in which we never step off the narrow path, never take the roads that lead us to the homes where our sisters are getting married, and where our brothers fall silent while talking about us while our grandmothers quietly wait for their grandsons to return so that they can sleep in peace? By now, my brother must be taller than his late father and (experiencing a tinge of happiness in his sad heart) must look exactly like him. And what about widowed and crazed mothers? God knows who looks after them. Oh my God, mercy, don't put our mad mothers on trial and let them die. (*No, relax, let them remain oblivious to all of this.*)

No, Janab-e-Aali, if our Constitution cannot provide us with a corridor through a foreign country to reach the graves of our people—who are as ours, as much our own, as we are to ourselves—at least we can create a corridor within our hearts where, heads lowered, when we open our palms in prayer, we should not be considered terrorists. What do terrorists have to do with pain and prayers?

I am alone and you are an entire constitutional system with its big army. How can I dare to challenge you? Only the individual will die in such an unequal battle. There is no room for a fight here. What is needed is the understanding that no human constitution should betray the demands of the natural order.

A thousand contradictions, hidden and overt, blend with each other simultaneously in the working of nature, and that is because nature does not shrug off its responsibility to sustain human beings. So the question is not simply of following the law, but of doing justice through the law. Through justice, gradually, we find the basis to identify individuals and things. That is why, when a prosperous society busies itself in revelry after a feast, God goes looking in the dark corners for those few who went to sleep on hungry stomachs. This caution is mandatory in democratic morality so that the Constitution does not break the heads of the oppressed like a blind man swinging a stick.

The applicant appeals that one should abstain from instigating any search for such unempathetic aspects of our Constitution. The collective misery of any nation is actually a manifestation of the sum total of the miseries of its individuals. Just think—when my grandmother, after years of desiring to embrace me, finally arrives at my doorstep, why should my reaching for her be considered something that makes us liable to arrest? Is it because she is the citizen of an enemy country? Are these countries each other's enemies, or are the residents of these countries enemies? Why? Because they are residents of an enemy country? If the residents are each other's enemies, then did my grandmother come here to murder me?

Janab-e-Aali, once, two brothers who had quarrelled divided their ancestral land between them and decided to live separately. It is a universal truth that cultivation on the bosom of the land must not be aborted, so that it can keep nurturing its sons and daughters. So, on the line that the two brothers drew, there sprouted some lost seeds of rice. This is what God's creation seeks—a spring everywhere and progeny playing and eating together. Tell me: what do you say about this truth?

You say *patriotism*? But who are fellow countrymen? The people you and I love naturally, obviously! Wherever these people may go, to England or Azerbaijan, they inhabit my heart. My wife, children, brothers and sisters, parents, and she—my real grandmother, in whose chest the fire of love burned all her life. We can relate with friends outside of our existence, and that is why we can make friends anywhere. But blood cells are only found in blood. Tell me—can I stand intact and complete without my family? No—why? Am I not the master of my existence? Janab-e-Aali, it is because wherever they may be during the day, members of a family return, without fail, to sleep at home at night. Our hearts burst into a storm if one of them does not return. So then, please explain to the applicant how he could break his relations with his people?

One of your intelligence officers once advised me: 'It is the demand of the love of your country that you should now forget everyone across the border. Live with only those who are really with you.' But the reason why human beings never really die is that those who vanish from sight can still be felt living in one's heart. That is why my dead father is alive, just like before.

(He continues despite losing his memory.)

Let me briefly narrate a real incident. Our ancestral village was on the border of a thick forest, spread over many miles. Plenty of different kinds of animals lived in this forest. Once, the forest caught fire and it quickly spread far and wide. In the confusion, the animals ran away, all in different directions. When the fire died, the forest was filled with the loud wailings of the animals who had found a refuge returning to find their near and dear ones who had been left behind...

Fortunately, animals do not have long memories. They forgot their kin in a few days and happily started living their isolated lives. But what should a poor human member of Noah's community do with the vigilant nail of memory fixed deep in his mind? Should it be pulled out? How? With memory is associated the human ego, because of which man has been placed on top of the universe. Think about it—if the applicant forgets the face of his lost sister, what difference will be left between him and a monkey? How will he remain civilised if his past is not offered to him in his future?

In my blood, I can hear the sound of horse's hooves from the past when my ancestor, in search of livelihood, came on a magical flying horse and entered India from Central Asia. He cried with happiness on seeing the beauty and food aplenty: *it is better than I imagined*! He got himself recruited in a local army near Delhi and married the first woman he saw, as though she were nature's gift. Dark as could be, but extremely beautiful! And he settled down here. What about returning? He knew there was no restriction on returning, so the thought of going back never crossed his mind. When there is no guard on the borders, we sit, unworried, within the four walls of our house. But if a member of the family is on the other side of the border, and there is a strict censorship even on news of their well-being, well then, kindly advise the applicant how he could escape from the sound of horse's hooves echoing in his blood? Why should his heart not wish to jump to the other side at the slightest opportunity?

Yes, undoubtedly, thanks to terrorism, life has become topsy-turvy on both sides of the borders.

But Janab-e-Aali, your problem is that professional terrorists are coming and going unchecked while the people being arrested are those who failed to resist their natural love; who suddenly decided to go from here to there. Just pause and reflect—does the compelling desire to embrace one's sister or mother make one a terrorist or an extremist? It will be a wonder if a person does not become a terrorist after being the constant target of the government's suspicion. After years of separation from my dear and near ones across the border, at last, I am getting to know about them... God forbid that they are dead and gone.

One cannot meet the dead unless one dies. Therefore, as a responsible citizen, I think I should impersonate a professional terrorist, and then I should move towards the border and, in the crossfire from both sides, leave my life there, and run like a crazy person and fall into the lap of my grandmother. No, Janab-e-Aali, I am a very life-loving person. But when life itself becomes death, then it looks as though we would come alive only after death, when we meet our dear separated ones and be at peace.

Janab-e-Aali, the applicant is desirous of forgiveness since he is unable to explain his point with legal expertise. Or, he is simply unable to articulate the reason why he has written this application. Under the circumstances, it is my respectful request that you prepare a legal draft of my sins yourself, and put it up for your own sympathetic consideration.

The clerks of the home departments of both Hind and Pak laughed uproariously after reading this application and, after stamping 'no action' on it, sent it to their respective head clerks. The head clerks brought to use all their experience and wisdom and arrived at the conclusion with a startle—this Mohammad Mustafa is definitely someone extraordinarily smart and clever; everything about this man ought to be investigated. Putting each application by Mustafa in a file marked 'Secret', each clerk moved towards the room of his respective boss. But outside the room of each senior hung a 'Do not disturb' plate. Inside, a stormy meeting was going on. In this meeting, the discussion revolved around providing the most modern weapons to security forces to crush such terrorists as him.

Sea of Breaths

(Saans Samundar)

'No, Ballu, my age is unchanged since the day I left. Was there even a chance to keep living after leaving this place?'

'Then how have you become so big and terrifying, you son-of-a-bhalu, a bear yourself!'

'Look, call me anything, but I'll smash your head if you call me a bhalu.' (He laughs and pulls his chair closer to himself.)

'Even now, you get irritated by your real name, Sheikh Mohammad Ikram. Alas, you have grown older but you haven't grown up.'

'Haan, yaar, that is what I tell you—I am still stuck in the same place. I have not been able to grow up, not even a bit. We can only grow up in a home. Have you ever seen the homeless growing up?'

'What is a home, Bhalu? The roof under which one lives with one's wife and children—that's home.'

'No, Ballu, you wouldn't know—a home is where the graves of our ancestors are in the same neighbourhood as us. Home is where, to offer fateha and express our fellowship with them, we walk at a leisurely pace, reach the street corner, and just one or two furlongs away, walking through a muddy path, we reach the graveyard…'

'Why are you weeping? I never ever saw any bhalu but you weep.'

'What was needed was to beat you Hindus up and send you off to Pakistan. You burn your elders and scatter them and then you are free to go anywhere. Why did we have to leave our ancestors behind, sleeping in their graves?'

'Don't worry, even now, your ancestors are sleeping peacefully as they were.'

'Don't lie, Ballu. Bhabhi was telling me yesterday that a cinema hall has been erected right across the middle of the graveyard.'

'So what, Bhalu? Whenever Dada jaani felt a little

anxious or nervous, he would make sure that the gatekeeper didn't catch sight of him, and he would go and sit in the deluxe class without buying a ticket.'

'Many a time have I thought about this, and, truly, what happened was for the best. At least we got rid of you kafirs.' Bhalu feels relaxed and reaches for the cup of tea on the table.

A man addicted to sinning keeps turning to look at hell.

'Your cup is empty, Bhalu. Wait, let me pour some tea in it.' While filling his own cup: 'Drink to your heart's content. Where would you find such good tea in Pakistan? Listen—the clouds are thundering out of season.'

'Do you remember, Ballu? Once, when we could not pay the tea bill for two months at the college canteen, the owner had reported the matter to the principal.'

'Yes, I remember clearly. The principal had fined us thirty rupees each. You had started pleading, "Sir, if we had the money, wouldn't we have paid the bill for the tea?" Here, have a samosa too—it has been pleading with folded hands, *please, stuff me in your mouth.*'

He picks a samosa from the plate and raises it towards his own mouth.

'Hey, Ballu, you wolf, you ask me to eat it but opened your own mouth!'

'So what? You take one, too—anyway, you people eat nothing but meat. Here's what you should do: for as long as you are here, at mealtimes, you should fly to your Pakistan.'

'No... I... me...'

'What me-me? Have you turned into a goat after having eaten loads of its meat?'

'No, baba, I have actually turned pure vegetarian.'

'Pure vegetarian? Haha! You are a complete fraud! My sister Shaily also used to say that you have become a pure vegetarian. After you two started an affair, I began to call her Rehmat Bi...'

'*Where is she now*? You are asking me as if you suddenly thought of her. Shaily is in Mumbai these days. *Who with?* With her husband and her numerous children, who have grown bigger than her. She is as fat as you are old now.'

'What nonsense are you talking about?'

'Precisely what you heard. Some just grow old, and some grow old and fat. Rehmat Bi has become so fat that if you stand near her you will be invisible. On hearing your trembly voice, she'd think you are talking from somewhere in Pakistan and then, after being happy for a short while, toss her head and return to her work.'

'Why doesn't Shaily try to do something about her size?'

'Why don't you try to do something about ageing? Be thankful that you don't have the visa to visit Mumbai. Her husband, with his long and broad arms jutting out from his sides, an unruly and narrow-minded Sardar, is very loud about his hatred of sexual excess.'

'Okay, give me all the details of Shaily's family.'

'Come on yaar, you Muslims know nothing other than amorous pursuits. Who knows how you are running your country, Pakistan.'

Outside, the thunder has grown louder. It is about to rain.

'You, who is putting so much effort in running Hindustan, tell me, has it even learnt walking after being fifty or fifty-five years old? Your samosa is very delicious, Ballu.'

'It is from Bangu Halwai's. He is a very talented sweet-maker. Just as you went over there after Partition, he stumbled across this way to come to the banks of the Triveni. He says he wasn't sure whether, after his death, his kids would have brought his ashes here or thrown them in some drain over there. But Bangu is a pure Punjabi, and his children have become so fluent in chaste Hindi living here that the poor man does not understand a word they say. Do your children understand your language, Bhalu?'

'One of my sons, Dr Ashraf, lives with me, one lives in America, and a daughter lives in England. None of them understands my language. I always speak to them by translating into English.'

'But your English was always very poor. Hai, hai! It has started drizzling. What do you know Bhalu? When I am talking to my children, I also speak in my Urdu-Hindi, even though I am not familiar with Hindi.'

'What? Is Urdu not foreign to you?'

'Hai, hai! Say what you want, yaarum, you are not wrong. The political parties over here issue all kinds of statements for or against Urdu—it is as if this language belongs only to the Muslims. Now the state of affairs is such that if I utter even one small thing from the heart, I feel as if I am preaching Islam.'

'This is good news. Maybe, in this way, you may in some time accept the right path. And following the right path, you'll find yourself in Pakistan. What a pleasure it would be if you reach there even by mistake! I always wait to welcome you. Over there, I see nothing around myself, only my Allahabad looms before my eyes.'

'You are very fortunate, Bhalu. At least there's something before your eyes. I can see only what is right in front of me—it is raining hard now—yes, you are really fortunate. These dirty lanes of Allahabad, where I walk cautiously, occupy my waking life, but somehow, what reaches your nose is their familiar fragrance. Oh! You've made a weepy face again.'

'You kaafirs drove us out from our paradise. I stay there, Ballu, but I live here, in Allahabad.'

'No, you stay there and you also live there. Don't cry, you win every move in the game with your weeping.'

'I have lost every move, Balua!'

'So what if you lost? At least you played every move.'

'When did I play? My life is stuck at the point before any move had been made!'

'No, however it is played, the game of life inevitably reaches its conclusion on its own.'

~

'Here, Bhalu (lighting a cigarette). Will you too smoke one? No? Why, you used to blow cigarette smoke from your mouth even in your dreams...'

'The doctor says that if you want to stay alive, don't even touch cigarettes.'

'Don't touch them (taking a long drag of his cigarette) that's the biggest life lesson... that life must be saved anyway, by keeping oneself away from cigarettes, or by leaving one's home during riots and taking refuge in Pakistan (takes another long drag). Look outside, it is raining heavily.

'Do you remember that day, Ballu? The riots had not yet started in Allahabad, but we were always afraid they would, and then one day, in the backyard of this very house, as we were playing cricket, I hit the ball so hard that your hands were suspended in the air like a bowl while the ball flew away and got lost, God knows where. And amidst all this, my brother came running, "*Chalo*! *Chalo*! *Bhaijaan*...".' (Let's go! Let's go! Brother...)

'Leave these stories, Bhalu. You have told them so often in your letters. Your Bhaijaan pulled you by the arm and took you to the edge of the lane where his car was waiting. *Chalo!* And as soon as you stepped into the car, you saw that your Bhabhi was sobbing and trying to console little Pappu in her lap, and Pappu's elder brother, Jammi, too, huddled fearfully on her other side.'

'Yes, I screamed and asked what has happened. *The rioters have set our house on fire*! Has the fire not been extinguished? *What hope is there of it being extinguished now*? Ballu, our car seemed to fly and my Abbu, Ammi, Dada jaan and Dadi-amma, all of them emerged from their graves and, without wings, silently followed our car. *Oh, cruel people. Oh! In whose care are you leaving us? Oh, take us with you to Pakistan*!

'Go on, weep!' Ballu takes his friend's hand in his own with great tenderness.

To recall sad moments in happy times makes one feel cleansed.

'No, yaar, Ballu! You say saving one's life is the greatest inspiration, but after saving it, one should be able to live one's life.'

'But that's what you do, Bhalu. That is why you are breathing, that is why you have built a new home, had children, and lived so long that you have grown old.'

'Yes, Bhai, one cannot but go on breathing involuntarily yet intensely, till death.'

Ballu stands, hearing the phone ring.

'Hello? Hello? Bhabhi? Yes, Ikram is sitting next to me. Yes, he is just coming. Come, Bhabhi has called you from Karachi.'

'Hello, Fatima. What? Oh no! I hope Ashraf does not have too many injuries. He's hospitalised! Don't worry, I will return home by the first flight today evening. No—what will I do here? *Allah hafiz.*'

'What has happened?'

'A bomb exploded outside Ashraf's dispensary, and he has also been injured.'

'How sad.' He puts his hand on his friend's shoulder and presses it.

'I want to go back, Ballu. If possible, right away.'

'Yes, of course.'

Oh! Tyrant—are you leaving without meeting us?

Outside, the grey clouds have lifted but it rains as before.

Grandmothers

(Dadiyaan)

Grandma's house was more than a hundred years older than even her. This is why, wherever she was in the house, she kept her head and forehead veiled. She lived by herself in the house. Eons ago, Grandpa had died. When death visited the house again, it did not even knock at the door but barged straight in and carried away her only son, Dhani Ram. Two years later, her daughter-in-law, too, followed her husband. Her grandson Ram Chand used to live with her but a few years ago, when he was allotted government quarters, he shifted there with his wife and children. Grandma dug her heels in, saying she wouldn't go anywhere leaving the house alone.

'Why would we abandon the house, Grandma, we will put it up for rent.'

'Very good, Ram Chanda, when the old are no longer of use, put them up for rent to earn money.' Granny straightened her bent back and looked him in the eye. 'I will not set foot outside this house. Why don't you put me up for rent along with it?'

There were nine rooms in Grandma's house. Of these, the roof had caved in three rooms. The third one might have remained standing, but some thief, expecting to steal goodness knows what from Grandma's house, started scaling the outer wall. The old house coughed several times to shoo away the thief, but he did not go away. So the wall risked its own life and suddenly collapsed on itself, and along with it the entire section of the roof covering the inner room also came down. Groaning over his injuries, the thief barely managed to escape.

Grandma was by herself, but she was so engrossed in herself that when she moved from one inner room to the other, she would find herself sitting there, waiting for herself.

'Grandma, you are still busy peeling the vegetables?'

'What to do, Grandma, I can hardly hold the brinjal. It slips out of my hands.'

'Give it to me. You are good for nothing now.'

'Why are you extending your hand that way if you want to hold it in your hand? The brinjal is here, in my right hand.'

'My eyes are no longer what they used to be, Grandma.'

'So what? How many more years do you now have left to keep seeing?'

'No, I want to be able to see till the time I stop breathing.'

By the time the two of them would get up and bring the diced vegetables into the kitchen, another Grandma would already be there, trying to light the stove.

'Come on, Grandma, move away, and here, give me the blower to light the fire!'

No, it was not as if Grandma was alone... or that she got lonely. Finishing so many household tasks was never work for a single person. Even so, she would get bone tired and come out to the courtyard for a break, and see herself already lying down, stretched tall across the string bed. She would get annoyed on seeing herself lying there.

'Grandma, hey Grandma! Have you gotten so old

that you are tired all the time and keep dozing off? Get up and let me lie down, I say.'

But then she would feel sorry for her—what else should the poor soul do?

Until she had a breath left in her body, Grandma would keep running around in all directions for some chore or another. Now, things have come to such a pass that she could do some work only if she could get herself up.

Grandma would seat herself next to the foot of the string bed and absent-mindedly start pressing her own aching feet. In the meantime, the grandma sleeping on the string bed would awaken and get up to sit next to her. 'Are you tired, Grandma? Here, let me press your feet.'

Grandma was over ninety now. This was the age when no matter how loud and clear the call of a koel was, it would fall on deaf ears. But many times, it so happened that Grandma could not fall asleep and, after midnight, a koel wandering outside in the moonlight—the same bird every time—would land on the peepal tree in her courtyard and, in a syrupy-sweet voice, call out to Grandma. Drops of warmed up oil would pour into Grandma's ears then, opening the clogged routes all the way to her heart.

'She's here!'

A number of grandmas would come up to stand around Grandma.

'Who?'

'Who else but our own Kesri?'

Kesri was Grandma's closest friend from her innocent girlhood days. Bathed in a beautiful dark hue, she always kept chattering in her birdsong voice.

'Bhagwan made you into a girl without thinking, Kesri,' Grandma would tell her friend. 'Look out, or one of these days, you will grow wings and fly all over the place like a koel.'

'Haan, and flying around, I'd land in the courtyard of your in-laws.'

But Kesri flew off and landed in the Seventh Heaven even before Grandma's wedding. In her married life, Grandma hardly even thought about Kesri, but on one recent night, all on her own, Kesri climbed down from the sky and sat on the mango tree in her courtyard. Hearing the sweet call ringing across from her childhood, Granny's dwindling hearing awakened, making her yearn to run back to her parents' village.

Back then, during weddings, Kesri would scoop up the black soot from the stove and paint huge moustaches on her face. She would then wear her dupatta like the turban men wear, and go to the women's area, playacting as the groom, struggling and fighting to remove the ghoonghat from Grandma's face, but Grandma won every time.

But Dhani Ram's father had removed Grandma's ghoonghat with one sweep of his hands, and turning red like the rain-beetle with her head and face bare, she had put her hands on her eyes, and while doing this, her hands jingled with the sound of her bangles, and then, 'Kooo. Koo!'

Hearing Kesri's call, Grandma felt as though she was the one sitting here in the inner room and also way over there. It was she, the flower bursting and blooming on the mango tree in the moonlight as well as Kesri, biting the fruit with her beak—'koo, kooo!'

'Arrey Grandma, where are you running to?'

'Come, Grandma. You, too, come along and join me.'

On the doors of all the inner rooms, grandmas collected and started peering over each other's shoulders. But outside, the moonless winter night was sheer darkness, so much so that the entire courtyard had dissolved into it and disappeared. Grandmas perked their ears; perhaps they would get to hear the fluttering of Kesri's wings, but there was not a sound except for the wailing of a cat far away.

Finding one grandma smiling, all the others, like her shadows, began to look just the same. 'How crazy I am, Grandma! The call rose from within my heart and instead I came running out!'

Not one or two but scores of birds had built their nests in Grandma's inner rooms. Wherever Grandma would step, birds would rise to create a kind of umbrella over her and begin to chirp loudly—'chirp, chirp-chirp, ch—'

'I haven't come here to listen to your chirpy sermon, girls. Tell me, where is my stone for grinding the spices?'

Chirping loudly, some birds would alight on the round grindstone lying in one corner and, not finding enough space to accommodate themselves, they would push and shove against each other.

'Yes, yes, I have seen the grindstone. Now get off it so I can hold it.'

'Chirp, chirp-chirp, ch—!'

'No, girls! I don't have time to waste in talking to you!'

'But Grandma, these talkative girls will not let you get up,' Grandma would say, and so, Grandma would sit down.

'O, Kaushalya, how is your young one doing now?'

Kaushalya's little one would hop down from the nest before his mother could open her mouth to chirp. 'I am all right, Grandma... look!' And he would, with one sweep of his wings, cover the entire roof.

'All right, don't show off now,' and Grandma would begin to search for the knot in her dupatta in which she kept a bit of rice for the birds. 'This is where I had kept it, Grandma. I hope it didn't come loose.'

'You are very firm in your knots, Grandma. How could it come loose?'

'Yes, here it is. I found it.'

Shifting the handful of rice from the knot into her clenched fist, she would be about to scatter it on the floor when the birds would swoop down to swallow it all. Birds in the other inner rooms would get wind of the ongoing feast and rush to join them in getting a mouthful. Seeing all the birds busy chirping, hopping, eating, Grandma would feel as though her faltering eyes mirrored their lively movements.

'Get up, Grandma. They are off to work, but all our tasks remain undone.'

Grandma knew that a very old snake had stationed itself in the last inner room of the house. On the very day after her bridal palanquin reached the home of her in-laws, she saw the snake coiled up, sleeping next to its hole. Seeing it, she had screamed in fear. Hearing her, her dear mother-in-law had come running there.

'What has happened, Bahurani?'

On seeing the snake, her mother-in-law quickly pulled her dupatta over her face. 'May you live long, Bahurani, may you bathe in milk and be the mother of many grandsons...'

It was Grandma's daily routine to fill a small bowl with milk and keep it next to the snake hole. The next morning, she would carry the emptied bowl back.

Some cat or another must be lapping it up, her Dhani Ram had once laughingly remarked. To atone for this comment by her husband, Grandma had offered food to five Brahmins. Cat or not cat, she never missed feeding this old ancestor of the household.

'One night,' Grandma would repeat a story she had told many times, 'I had such high fever that I fainted. How would I serve milk to the Mahan Sasur Raja (great father-in-law) of mine? Close to midnight, I became conscious and felt that my fever was lower.

My body felt light as I have never felt it even when fully healthy. I realised suddenly that I had not served my Sasur Raja his milk. I got up with a start and suddenly saw Mahan Sasur Raja standing in one corner with his hood spread wide. I immediately pulled my ghoonghat down and folded my hands to offer greetings to him. I don't know how long he had been looking after me. When he turned away to go to his room, I ran to the kitchen to fetch his milk bowl.'

Grandma was not alone, yet sometimes, her heart brimmed over and she would wade into its deep waters and wonder where all the people had gone—they were lost, as if in some labyrinth, gone forever, never to show their faces again. In the monsoon, when the roof of the old house started leaking, she would speak out: 'Do you see, Grandma? This house was our only ancestor who stood tall and firm. Now he, too, is cracking up and crying.'

'Don't worry, Grandma. We are just the same,' the house would respond.

'How are we just the same? When I want to hold you to my breast to feel light and relieve myself from the burden of my sorrows, all I can do is to pull at my own chest. Tell me, is this how one must live?'

'But what to do, Grandma?' Grandma said to Grandma. 'Till your breathing stops, there is no recourse but to go on living.'

'This is why I continue to live.'

Today, too, was a day like that and dark, heavy clouds of memories hovered around Grandma's mind. Memories of her near and dear ones, and clouds impatient to burst forth any minute... On such occasions, Grandma would gather all the other grandmas around her. They would all pull down their ghoonghats and start lamenting in their congregation.

Dragging her body with great difficulty, Grandma pulled herself to the innermost room. All the other grandmas followed her, and when she sat on the floor and lowered her dupatta, all of them sat around her, pulled down their dupattas, and started wailing in the same tune:

'O mother of mine!'

'O Mother, my near and dear one!'

'Come, my mother!'

'Come and see your daughter Dhanno crying!'

'Come and skim the cream from the milk and put some in my mouth!'

'Come on, nobody is here who will catch us!'

'Come, why are you quarrelling with your sisters-in-law?'

'Come, wipe the tears from your child's eyes!'

Grandma lifted the ghoonghat from her face and spoke to all the grandmas, 'How can you be so unemotional? Come on, cry louder!' Then she pulled the ghoonghat over her head, so low that the snow-white hair on the back of her head began to show.

'O father of mine!'

'Dear Father, oh Father!'

'You were lame, yet you carried me all over the village.'

'How you loved me, village headman!'

'Oh, but you loved your honour even more than me!'

'For the sake of honour, you handed me over to strangers.'

'Raised on the choicest milk, this honey-like daughter of yours ... you handed her over to strangers.'

'Hai, headman! Hai!'

'Hai, hai, Father!'

Like the roof, Grandma's eyes began to drip drop.

'Now who would oil your head, oh Father!'

'My brothers would go and be with their wives

as soon as they came home, and mother was tied to household chores.'

'Who would tie bandages on your legs?'

'Why did you hand me over to the strangers?'

'Hai! Hai, Father, hai!'

Beating her breast, Grandma got up, and when she could no longer stand, she sat down.

'Hai, Dhani Ram's Bapu, hai, you really turned out to be a stranger.'

'You were my good luck, Bapu!'

'Hai, he took my hand and he abandoned me, Dhani Ram's Bapu!'

'Hai, Bapu, your umbrella got left behind in the house.'

'Where did you go in such heavy rain, Bapu?'

'Hai, Sasuma, you called your son away from me on the sly!'

'Hai, mother-in-law, if only you had called me too. I would have seated you on a throne and washed your feet.'

'Sons don't serve their mothers, daughters-in-law do!'

'Hai, my only lion!'

When Grandma thought of Dhani Ram, water

dripping from the roof began to fall upon all the grandmas' heads.

'I had only one lion, good people, only one!'

Who knows from where Grandma got this power to cry out, beat her breast, and shake her body.

'Hai, my Dhania, the lion!'

The other grandmas could no longer accompany Grandma. First, they stared at her and when they could no longer bear to see her suffer so much, they moved towards her to quieten her.

'Enough, Grandma, enough!'

'Come on, my lion, I have made kheer for you.'

'Enough!'

'Come on, son! Come!'

Grandma spread her hands wide open and then pulled them to her bosom as if she was holding her little Dhania in her arms.

She quietened for a while to gain control of her palpitating breaths.

'Where were you lost, Dhania?'

'Enough, Grandma, enough!'

'Shshshsh!' Grandma was regaining her composure.

'Can't you see, Grandma, the baby's just gone to sleep?'

Grandma kept quiet and the water from the roof also stopped dripping.

Then Grandma and the grandmas sat in silence and when the sun began to shine again, Grandma pulled her dupatta over her head. Looking at her face, one could see that she had gone and met all her near and dear ones to her heart's content.

'Arri Grandma,' she stood up abruptly. 'Stones must have fallen upon my brain that I left the already cooked meal on the lit stove.'

She rushed with such alacrity towards the door that all the other grandmas could only watch her.

To reach the kitchen, she had to pass through the inner courtyard. In her blind rush, when Grandma came to two small steps in the verandah facing the inner rooms, her foot skipped the first and fell on the edge of the second one. She fell on her face in the courtyard and till her last breath, she kept thinking about the meal burning to cinders on the stove.

Sitting in the new township six miles away from the old city, how would Ram Chand have known what had happened here? Before anyone else, it was the bitch who used to come to Grandma to get her daily roti who understood everything that had transpired.

The doors of Grandma's old home were much higher than the ground level. Like every other day, the bitch slipped from under the partially closed door, and finding Grandma sprawled on the floor, she began to bark. She ran around Grandma a couple of times as if she could not understand what had happened and what must be done next. Then she made up her mind and began running towards Ram Chand's quarters.

Ram Chand didn't know what the dog was trying to convey at first, but after a long time, he began to recognise her and understood. He ran with her towards Grandma's home. Perhaps Grandma had passed away, and he felt a pang: he had been angry with her just before he had left; somebody should have been with her in her last hours.

'It's fine, Grandma, if you don't want to come with us, don't!'

'But why don't you live here with me?'

'No, Grandma. Now you can live here all by yourself!'

Ram Chand's servant would bring her supplies regularly every month. But let alone a human being, not even an animal can survive just on food, living by itself. Running to the house, he was panting from fatigue but also from remorse. If Grandma had really died, then how could stone-hearted he be alive?

The rickety door came crashing down after some pulling and pushing, and with it fell Grandma's grandson. He had barely managed to get back on his feet when Grandma's Mahan Sasur Raja, with his hood spread wide, greeted him with a hiss and slithered off down some crevice. Ram Chand was trying to get back to his senses but turning into the courtyard, he froze. In the glowing light of the full moon, Grandma's dead body lay in the middle of a circle with grandmas and grandmas all around.

Hunger Demons

(Bhook Pret)

Stop, Brother!

Stopped, brother!

Let me cry a little before you tell more of your tale.

Why just a little, Brother? Cry with total abandon.

No, Brother. If I cried with complete abandon, you would forget your tale.

Yes, if I forget the tale, what would I tell?

But your tale has reached such a happy climax, Brother, that my tears refuse to stop flowing.

Yes, Brother. He who cries a little in moments of happiness can laugh during sadness.

No, if you proceed with such a preoccupation with death, you will ruin your Judgement Day.

That is already ruined, Brother.

Tell me the complete story, Brother. You have already told me the ending.

Yes, once the entire story has played out, all that is left is telling it—so, what happened next, Brother, is that the Princess put her arms around my neck. The servants then moved the rulers' throne from its spot and positioned it behind us. And there we reclined, on the throne, ready to express our love…

Stop, Brother.

Stopped, Brother.

I feel like crying when I think about why all this didn't happen to me.

Neither do you cry, Brother, nor do you let the tale proceed.

Your story has already reached where it was meant to. Here, have this date if you are hungry…

This is a very tasty date, Brother.

Yes, here, have this water too.

Very sweet water too, Brother—now I will resume my story.

It has already reached here.

Where?

In this desert where we sit.

Yes, Brother. Wait, let me also cry a bit.

You put your head in your Princess's lap, and I will keep mine in your lap, and cry with all my might.

Wait, Brother, first let me rest my head somewhere. Then you can make your space in my lap—but what is this, Brother? You don't have a lap.

Yes?—Oh, yes—My lap, Brother?

Try to remember your full story, Brother. Try to remember—where did you leave your lap?

Where else? On the throne of the rulers under the Princess's head.

And you readily forgot it there?

Yes, I did forget it, Brother! The Princess's hair was so thick that I couldn't find it while getting up.

This is really bad, Brother!

Yes, it is bad, Brother.

Now the only way is to find the Princess! If your own lap is not with you, what would you live for?

I will live somehow, Brother.

But how, Brother?

Yes, how will I live?

If you wish to live, find your lap.

Where do I look, Brother?

On the throne of the rulers!

The magical throne of the sovereigns repels anybody who approaches it.

Then find the servants who can position the throne behind you to rest your back.

Those servants are in the Palace of the Princess.

And the Palace of the Princess?

It is in my thoughts, Brother…

And where are your thoughts, Brother?

They are close to me, but I do not know where.

If they are close to you, Brother, then they must be near you.

If I don't know where they are, Brother, who knows where they could be?

Stop, Brother.

Stopped, Brother.

If even your thoughts are lost to you, then why worry about what else you have lost?

Yes, Brother, you speak the truth.

Then carry on with your tale full throttle.

How do I carry on, Brother? It has reached where it had to.

Yes, this desert.

Yes, Brother, now it is only possible that I go back to get here again.

Yes, for who knows what lies ahead.

Yes, Brother, who knows what has still not come to pass.

Stop, Brother.

Stopped, Brother.

I know what will happen to us in the future.

What will happen, Brother?

We will get out of this desert.

Then come, Brother, let us proceed.

No, Brother, you retreat, because you came from the rear.

And you, Brother?

I came from nowhere, Brother. So I will go forward without further ado.

Won't you feel scared of strangers?

No, Brother, I don't know anyone, therefore, I don't perceive anyone as a stranger.

Then come, Brother. Let us turn our backs to each other and start off briskly on our own journeys.

Yes, come.

Stop, Brother.

Stopped, Brother.

Where are you coming from?

From the Palace of the Princess.

Astonishing!

No, Brother, what is so astonishing? By mistake, my face was turned this way and yours that way.

But I am also returning from the Palace of the Princess.

Astonishing!

No, Brother, what is so astonishing in this? This path must also lead to the Palace of the Princess.

Yes, it must lead there, Brother. Or else, how would you have reached there?

Yes, all roads lead to the Palace of the Princess.

Yes, even those we have not yet travelled.

Yes, take any road, and you would reach there.

Yes, Brother, return from any road.

Yes, Brother, but do return.

Yes, or we'll be separated.

No, we've just returned. Don't speak of separation.

Yes, if we mention separation, how will we be united?

Yes, speak of union—have you met my Princess?

Yes, I have met her, Brother—

Stop, Brother.

Stopped, Brother.

First tell me—

No, first listen to me, Brother—your lap was lying there, covered under the Princess's hair. I picked it up quietly, but when I was leaving, I forgot my own lap there.

Oh, no! It means I have brought your lap back as mine.

You are lying in my lap, Brother, that is why you appear so nice to me.

And you to me, Brother.

And, lying in each other's laps, we have reached heaven.

Yes, Brother, this oasis took a thousand steps to get here. And the servants have laid the sovereign throne behind us.

No, Brother. Do not look behind you, or this magical throne will throw you off again.

Yes, if we let go of our thoughts, we will be worth nothing.

What is the harm even if we are thrown off, Brother?

Yes, if thrown off our own thoughts, the notions of profit and loss lose meaning…

Forget profit or loss, Brother. Here—have this date.

A very tasty date, Brother.

Yes, here, have this water.

Very sweet, Brother.

Yes, now sleep, Brother.

I am very sleepy, Brother.

Stop, Brother.

Stopped, Brother.

If we sleep, who will wake us up?

He who puts you to sleep also wakes you up.

Come then, let us sleep.

Yes, brother, let us sleep.

Have you fallen asleep, Brother?

No, Brother, I am thinking about the Princess.

But I sense you are asleep.

Yes, Brother, the Princess's hair is so thick that it feels like one is asleep.

Yes, Brother, and her face is so pure that even when drowned in sleep, it feels as if we haven't reached its depths.

Yes, we keep seeing her even in our dreams.

Yes, and she sees us.

Yes, if we sleep, our fate looks up.

Yes, in our dreams, silver dust falls on us from the moon.

Come, Brother, let us quietly sleep.

Yes, come—no, not here, there.

Yes, sleep is awake over there.

Yes, if it is awake, it won't let thieves in.

Stop, Brother.

Stopped, Brother.

Hunger is stroking my liver again.

So have this date, Brother, or hunger will eat your liver.

Very tasty date, Brother.

Here, have this water, Brother.

Very sweet water, Brother.

Yes, now sleep.

Yes, now the doors of the eyes are closing without having to try.

Yes, now it is time, Brother, to enter the domain of sleep.

But if the doors shut, Brother, how will you get out?

Brother, if we don't enter, how will we get out?

Yes—goodnight, then, Brother!—I'm off.

Yes, go.

Yes, I'm off.

You are back again, Brother? You hadn't even left but have already returned?

Thank God, Brother, that I have returned, otherwise, who can return after travelling thousands of miles in a moment?

Yes, God be thanked, you have returned, but where had you gone, Brother?

Nowhere, Brother. I was with the Princess, about to take off from the sovereign throne. But as I was taking flight, I heard you calling. Cursing you, I stepped down from the throne, and it was as if I was still on the ground.

But you were in the air.

Yes—where else?

Then it is better that you returned to the ground, Brother. Since God did not give us wings, it is better that we lie on the ground.

But there is no sleep on the ground, Brother.

Yes, or if it comes, there is always the fear that we can no longer open our eyes.

Stop, Brother.

Stopped, Brother.

Hunger is troubling me again.

So what, Brother, here—have this date.

Very tasty date, Brother.

Here, have this water, Brother.

Very sweet water, Brother.

If your stomach is full now, then begin the tale, Brother.

Should I begin my tale of the Princess?

Yes, Brother.

If you allow me, Brother, shall I reveal the truth right down to the last letter?

Yes, Brother, it is God's commandment to always speak the truth.

The truth, Brother, is that I have always lied for my own happiness.

Which is why God has thrown you into this endless desert.

Yes, Brother, and you, too.

Yes, Brother, me too—here, have some more dates, you are going crazy with hunger.

Take this fistful of sand away, Brother, and let me sleep.

Yes, Brother, even if you fall asleep and don't wake up, which date will show up anyway?

Chance Encounters

(Mele Mulakatein)

On the frontiers of Wagah and Attari, a piece of land a few feet wide is no man's land. It is as if this land, still wrapped in a sheet after seeing the frightening dreams of 1947, is muttering, 'Na baba, I neither belong to Hindustan nor Pakistan. I do not belong to anyone and no one is mine.' It appears as if the momentary madness of her children has made the mother go mad forever. Her consciousness was injured by the repeated attacks of knives, lances, and axes, and she lost her memory: 'No one is mine. Na baba, I belong to no one.'

On the edges of both sides of this land flap the flags of Hindustan and Pakistan, facing each other. Below them stand two Punjabi sentries, humbly positioned.

The two strangers, Hindustani and Pakistani, so close to each other and yet so distant, remain quiet and tense. But their shadows, cast over their shoes, shake relentlessly as they keep trying to meet. Observing the sentries, one would think they have no name, or parents, nor neighbours—they are merely sentries. They only have numbers, which, if they forget them, then the whole world might refuse to recognise them. Perhaps they may even lose recognition of themselves.

'You have become someone else,' the mother of his children had said tearfully, when the Pakistani sentry had gone home on leave the last time.

'Yes, now I will be promoted to Hawaldar.'

Twirling his moustache on the right side, the Pakistani sentry contemplated. If only he'd get an opportunity to risk his life on the frontier, he would be made Hawaldar in days. But what can one do? There doesn't seem to be any possibility of a skirmish as of now.

On the other side, the Indian sentry fixed his eyes on a group of people coming towards him with the intention to cross into Pakistan from the Hindustan border.

'They appear to be Pakistanis.'

'No, they are Hindustanis.'

'Why are these people going to Pakistan now?' (The Hindustani sentry would be very surprised on seeing Hindustanis going to Pakistan.)

'To eat the bloody red malta grown on that side!' He had seen the Pakistani sentry peeling a third and then a fourth malta since morning.

'No, you cannot carry even a single banana from the Indian frontier,' he had said very sternly to a traveller passing across the border.

In the meantime, a child from among the people going to Pakistan came running, carrying a stray puppy, and reached the Hindustani sentry.

'Stop!'

The puppy jumped out of the boy's grasp, barked at the sentry, and crossed the border but the human child stood back, afraid.

'Passport.'

After showing their passports, the group stepped into the no man's land.

One man from the group began to say, 'The gates of both frontiers are opened at sunrise and closed at sunset.'

'The security here is very tight.'

They all stopped and looked this way and that.

A man who looked like a professor gestured towards the entire area and said, 'This piece of land belongs to God and not to man. It is just like in olden times when the entire earth belonged to God. Over here, there are no laws governing our living and dying, we are free like cats and dogs, we do not need any passport.'

'You are right. Man is truly a fool. He has needlessly bound this beautiful land of God with his petty laws.'

'Why do you consider these laws petty?'

'Because they have divided the human race by drawing lines over and over again. First, they drew hundreds of lines on the earth. Then they stuck separate flags on each of them. But underneath it all, people are one. And journeying along through life, we find that the soul of the entire earth is unified, its appearance is the same, and its very way of being is the same…'

'Haan, bhai, you are right. Once, while taking in the smell of the soil of a field in England, involuntarily, the smell of the soil of my homeland had entered my nostrils.'

'Daddy, didn't you say the bull always carries the

earth on one horn? And when it gets tired, the…'

'Passport, please?' The Pakistani sentry stopped them.

When they had moved on after showing their passports, the Hindustani and Pakistani sentries stared at the traveller's backs for a long time. Suddenly, their gazes collided, just the way two strangers bump into each other in a crowd and who, without looking at each other, grumble and then go their separate ways.

Actually, the Hindustani sentry had seen the Pakistani sentry's face and the Pakistani sentry had seen the former's face too, but they did not recognise each other in the slightest. The truth is that their faces were invisible, even though their expressions had all the familiar features—the shadows of grief, the light of pleasant joys, and the marks of small domestic concerns. Both sentries had covered their real faces with icy, soldierly faces. They were cold faces, which, if one desired to kiss, one's lips would dry up, and which, if one desired to fling abuses at them, would make one tongue-tied. They are people one could neither love nor hate. These cold faces are all alike, just like the uniforms of sentries. How then was it possible to recognise their individual features?

After some time, an old woman came to the Pakistani border and stood near the sentry. She appeared restless and lost, and her voice was high-pitched.

'Beta, I want to go to Hindustan.'

The Pakistani sentry looked at her passport and, without looking at the Hindustani sentry, gestured towards him.

'Go.'

The old woman immediately went to the Hindustani sentry.

'Beta, I want to go to Hindustan.'

While looking at her passport, the Hindustani sentry said, 'This is Hindustan.'

The woman turned and looked at the Pakistani sentry, who was standing so indifferently a few feet away that it was as if he were a thousand miles away.

'No, beta, I am talking about Hindustan.'

'Which is your Hindustan, Mai ... ?' As the old woman's passport was Pakistani, the Hindustani sentry's voice had a touch of sarcasm.

'Saharanpur, where my daughter lives.' The old woman began to wipe her eyes with her dupatta. 'I am going to meet her for the first time since the creation of Pakistan.'

She appeared to be talking to herself. 'My son and I came from there.'

'Okay, go,' the sentry said, returning the passport to her.

'At what time does the train for Saharanpur leave?'

'Mai, you can inquire at the Amritsar station.'

'Where is the Amritsar station, son?'

It appeared that that the old lady was determined to meet her daughter once before dying, even if it meant persistently asking the way until she landed on the other end of the world.

'Where is the Amritsar station?' The aged mother's voice was calling out to her absent daughter in a beseeching tone.

A warm, pulsing drop of human blood created a tremor in the heart of the snowman and his icy face began to melt, and the misty face of the son of a mother appeared beneath his frozen features.

'Maa—' the sentry appeared to be addressing his own old mother. 'Some rickshaw-wallah will take you straight to the station.'

When his sister would not visit her parents' place in a long time, the cawing of crows would bring tears to his mother's eyes.

'Okay, son.'

When the absent-minded old woman turned her back, the soldier wished to follow her to help, but the burden of his gun and uniform kept him standing in his spot. He thought of his mother who has been living with his brother in a village in Bengal since five years. Before Pakistan was created, he, his mother, his sister, and his brother lived together in a village in Western Punjab. But after coming here, they were all scattered far away from each other and now they would sometimes—but only in their thoughts—meet each other in the courtyard of their old house.

'Maa!' the sentry's eyes were still fixed on the trembling shoulders of the old woman, as if he were an innocent child, and this mother was just going to visit neighbours, leaving him playing in the courtyard of their old house.

'Balwant Singh, son, keep playing over here.'

But Balwant Singh had come very far away while playing in the courtyard, and his weeping mother had reached some distant village in Bengal.

'Attention!' Who knows where from the sentry's officer had made a sudden appearance.

'Guard! Be alert. You have not been sent here to

sleep in your mother's lap. The border is a serious matter.'

'Yes, sir!' It appeared as if the officer had seen the sentry stark naked. He hastily pulled up his trousers and stood at attention.

In the meantime, the dog was spotted again, returning from the Pakistan border. The Pakistani sentry, with great swiftness, attempted to block its path, and was even about to utter 'passport!' but stopped himself midway. The dog responded with strange, unfamiliar sounds. It appeared as if it was unable to hold back its laughter.

The sentry wanted to kick it, but when it looked at him and wagged its tail in a friendly manner, he changed his mind and began to watch the dog's face with interest.

The human and the animal attempted to recognise each other for a few moments.

'What do you want?' the human's eyes asked.

Looks like a decent human. I can speak to him. The animal appeared harmless, mischievous, and petulant.

The human calmed down, and with a smile, he began to pat the animal's back.

Now I understand. The animal wagged its tail and came closer to him.

'Why do you come here?' The sentry was reminded of his Subedar's beautiful bitch. 'You bastard, have you fallen for our Subedar's bitch?'

The sentry twirled his moustache, felt a tickle, and began to laugh helplessly. Perhaps a scene from his Mamu's well in his village, near which he had seen a dog and a bitch glued to each other, had risen before his eyes.

'Shabash! You are a true lover. You manage to get across even from under the shadow of guns and rifles.'

The sentry began to remember those old days; the mother of his Noora was still a virgin. The maiden's beauty was like an earthen pot overflowing with water that kept spilling out. Instead of springing into some thirsty Jat's mouth, it fell to the earth.

'Hee-ha...Hee-hee!' On one Shab-e-barat, he had, in his madness, caught hold of the girl's wrist. Instead of becoming angry, she had laughed, and it was as if countless colourful cascades of stars had burst forth from an anar cracker.

The snowman, buried under layers and layers of ice, stood at the mouth of his old cave. But lying down on the warm and soft bed of his youth had sent rejuvenating warmth creeping into his icy body.

'Shere, if you pass by here again, we will break your legs!' The brothers of his Noora's mother had often threatened him.

Once, he was badly caught in their trap. If his friend Bhalu had not reached in the nick of time, they would have cut him to pieces with their knives. That day, Bhalu took a severe beating; the poor thing was completely soaked in blood.

'Bhalu!' Today, after a very long time, the sentry had remembered his Sikh friend. Bhalu appeared to be covered with hair from head to toe. The scoundrel was a bear in his entirety. If the village girls sighted his naked body, they would close their eyes out of fear. Noora's mother was also afraid of his funny friend. After his marriage, Bhalu joined the army, and after that, who knows where he had disappeared. After he married Noora's mother, he did not have any regret about parting with his old friend; he wanted to be close to Noora's mother all the time. It appeared as if Noora's mother was his wheat crop, and he was restless to harvest the entire field in one day.

The Pakistani sentry was still patting the dog lovingly on its back and the dog was sitting near him, licking his military boots.

'You have turned into somebody else.'

Now he felt that Noora's mother had been right to complain. He pledged to himself that when he went home on leave this time, he would take the pure 'Kunji Maar' brand dye for her hair.

The Peer Sahib's Sarai was built a long time back, but on Eid every year, after a whitewash, she appears like a new bride who has just been lifted off the mare.

'Oh! Have some patience.'

But he wanted to kiss the middle-aged mother of Noora in front of everybody on Eid…

When the dog saw the sentry talking to himself, he began to scratch his back with his hind leg and quietly made his way towards the Subedar's quarters.

After a while, the Pakistani sentry lifted his head and looked at the sun. There was still a little time before the gates closed. Turning his head, his eyes collided with the eyes of the Hindustani sentry again. They muttered something and then, in accordance with their daily routine, they stood erect, guarding the place. And then they conducted a routine that felt as though they were conversing with each other:

'Hain?'

'Haan!'

'One. Two. Three. Four…' The Hindustani sentry was counting his footsteps.

'Two. Three. Four…' The Pakistani sentry was also counting his footsteps.

'Where is your village?'

'There!'

'Where?'

'In Pakistan, where you live.'

'But Pakistan is my country.'

'It is my country too.'

'One. Two. Three. Four…'

'Two. Three. Four…'

The sentries kept counting their footsteps while their footsteps kept talking amongst themselves.

A short distance off, in the canteen at the Hindustani border, a song on the legendary Heer started playing on the loudspeaker. '*Heer akhdi jogiya jhooth aakhey…*' (Heer says the ascetic tells lies…)

Both sentries halted in the middle of their marching, involuntarily deafened by the sound and perplexed.

O Jogi! You lie; for who can pacify a sulking friend? I have searched everywhere, but found no person who can bring back the departed…

Heer's tearful voice pierced the border of

Hindustan and entered Pakistan, announcing that she was the voice of entire Punjab. You cannot enclose her within borders. You cannot put sentries to guard her. You cannot stop her from crossing into your border. Pakistani Punjab as well as Hindustani Punjab were listening to that voice, booming in all four directions.

Listening to that voice, the crazy no man's land began to feel that its memory was returning. The sentries just stood, bewitched, their hearts beating to one rhythm. The daughter of Punjab had united the feelings of both Punjabis on common ground.

The one who can cure our ailing hearts has the right to fashion shoes with our skins. Who knows when the true God will bring the departed ones' home...

The Punjabi sentries appeared to have got a glimpse of the poet Waris Shah descending from the skies and their hearts and souls embraced.

If I hear of Waris Shah's coming, I would light lamps with ghee, crumble bread for him to eat.

After Heer finished lamenting, both sentries glanced at each other and felt a jolt of recognition. Then they looked again at each other with deeper understanding.

'Shere.'

'Bhalu!'

Both friends called out to each other at the same time.

'Oye…tu?' (Hey…is it you?)

'Tu!' (You!)

For the last three days, these two friends who had grown distant had been on duty at the same spot. But they had not looked at each other. They had not recognised each other. Now their hearts raced with the longing to embrace, while their arms reached out… The setting sun wanted to stop and watch the scene of their reunion, but just then, the screaming Hindustani and Pakistani sirens announced that the gates of both borders would be closed immediately.

Outside In

(Bahar ke Bheetar)

It is an insignificant matter. He has to just go from here to there.

The road is about hundred feet wide and he stands on the footpath on one side, nervously wags his tail, and stares at the far side. Scores of vehicles zoom over the road at deadly speeds. It is but a matter of a few steps. If he were to step on the road, eyes shut, and if only those travellers rushing to and fro stopped for a while, too, he would silently cross the road without having to look to the left or right. Silently? As in, no one would even notice that he has crossed the road and reached the other side. But how would that happen? Is it that life would momentarily pause—as if a two-headed python were pulling it in opposite directions, draining all its strength, forcing it to stay in one spot—but that would be the end of the world, Doomsday. This helpless fellow is, after all, just a dog, not an avatar who can go from this side to the other in the midst of such a catastrophic doomsday.

The son of a dog still stands there. But he feels as though he has actually stepped onto the road and, leaving himself there, first sprung back and then returned to stand at the very spot where he had stood before. He pants, but is unable to hear his own panting. He has a strong wish to bark out aloud, but he has forgotten how to bark. Maybe he is barking, or maybe he is not, he doesn't know, since he has left himself by the road.

Then the dog feels that unless he perceives himself fully, he may lose the bolster of uncertainty and, becoming weightless, float up, lift off the earth. So he runs on his four legs until he reaches a corner of the same footpath where someone of his ilk had just peed. Sniffing an impression of himself in the wet soil, he feels relieved and, detecting himself as alive, barks happily. He was still barking when a beggar sitting under a tree threw a stone at him with great force, breaking his leg. But a strong desire to keep running heals him, and he runs on ahead, forgetting that he has to cross the road—go from here to there.

This road runs for twenty-four hours a day; it is, after all, made of cement and stone. Had it been made of flesh and bone, it would have slept for at least two or four hours a day. Nobody knows where the road leads to and where it begins, but since all of it is eternally on the run, it is always with itself—always—it is never out of its place either. This road stays where it is as innumerable wheels, speedily, perpetually, circle it.

~

Arrey bhai, wait! Where are all of you going?

We don't know where.

I don't know either.

Me neither!

But I know, come with me. Come!

Where to? Where are you going?

I don't know. We got lost. So if you really want to help us, tell us: have you ever seen us here before? Have you ever heard about us? Do you recognise us? Speak fast, or else leave, get out of our way; or get crushed under us.

Maybe... Oh, yes! Is it that we stopped ourselves

here one day and we crushed ourselves as we passed by? Yes, this is what might have happened. That's definitely what happened. And then? Then our bones were toughened by the repeated crushing, and this road may have been built with those very bones. But maybe, just maybe, that is not what happened, and we are still safe. If we are, then we may still be found somewhere on this road. So, come!

~

Still running along that roadside, it strikes the dog that he has left the butcher's shop behind. It is not evident whether the smell of the raw meat reached this spot, or if it lingered in the dog's head and only reached his nostrils when he got here. But he thinks about turning and going back, towards the butcher's shop. Just then, he sees a domesticated bitch before him and…and a strange thing happens—his front legs start taking him towards this bitch while his hind legs start moving towards the butcher's shop. Oh, God! Is he still the same dog, or two men?

And then he hits the track leading to the butcher's shop.

'Come in—what would you like? Tongue of goat, leg of chicken, ribs of sheep?'

'I have no money.'

'Stand aside then! Go away!' The butcher waves the sharp side of his long blade towards the dog's neck, so carelessly that if the dog had not moved quickly, his fresh meat, too, would be displayed on the shelves of the shop.

But the dog has already stuck his head into one shelf and started savouring his own meat, losing himself in his own head. The butcher throws a sharp bone on his back, which he grabs in his mouth and runs off, while yelping something about not letting the bone fall from his mouth.

And that is how he lands up here.

'Beat him! Beat him more! More! Shave his head, blacken his face, and put him on the back of an ass!'

'To hell with this damn dog!'

The dog bursts into laughter hearing that a dog would be made to ride a donkey.

'The shameless fellow is laughing! Beat him, hit him more!'

'What is the matter?'

'What does it have to be, sir? I went into this shop and my wife stood here—isn't it, darling?'

'Yes, I stood right here, waiting for my husband,

and this dog crept up from behind me and put his hands on my shoulders.'

'Hands on a dog? Madam may have mistaken its forelegs as hands.'

'Beat him, beat him to pulp!'

Despite the thorough thrashing, the dog's four limbs are safe and sound, and he feels sympathetic towards a helpless, disabled fakir he has spotted.

The fakir seems pleased when he notices the dog observe him keenly.

The fakir thinks: 'Even those who hand me a paisa or two don't look at me this way, and those who abuse me don't even bother looking at me. So much so, even I don't consider it worth my happiness to look at myself. "Always bring joy to the fakir, Madam, and God will bring you happiness," I say. *Hatt teri*! The stupid woman sees none but herself. If I had any money, I would throw ten thousand rupees at her and order her to kiss my dirty, ugly face in public lovingly. If ten thousand is not enough then take this—more—take more! But see me and smile.'

The dog smiles, and the fakir beckons him: 'Come, sit on my lap.'

The dog goes and sits next to the fakir, his tail wagging in the fakir's legless lap.

'Here, eat this,' and the fakir opens his cloth sack in front of the dog's face, and they eat together. 'It is tasty, na, isn't it?'

The dog pushes the fakir's hand away from his mouth and says, 'Let me eat first.'

The fakir's bag empties in a trice but they both continuously chew with empty mouths. Then, whoever got the idea first—the fakir's mind or the dog's head—stops chewing and stares at the other, and then the other also stops chewing.

'Go away, you wretch—will you eat my bones too?' The fakir pushes the dog's wagging tail off his lap, and it runs away, howling, then stops at a little distance and turns to look at the fakir. Was this gentlemanly behaviour?

'Get away, you son of a gentleman.' The fakir throws a stone at him, which he thought was a leftover piece of roti, and approached it. After a sniff at it, he barks at the fakir, 'Your mother's—! Your sister's—!'

'Get lost!' One after another, the angry fakir throws three or four stones at the dog, but he doesn't care, and just walks off until reaches a pedestrian crossing.

Life rolls past wildly on the opposite ends of the road.

~

Where are you going?

To where you came from. And what about you?

To where you came from.

But there is nothing there.

That is strange. There's nothing where I came from either.

There must be something!

No, nothing at all. If something were there, wouldn't I know it?

How is it possible that there is nothing at all where you have come from?

If you insist, there may be something and I may not have learnt of it.

Yes, maybe even I didn't come to know.

~

From the faces of the people waiting at the pedestrian crossing, one can sense that their souls have already crossed the road and, from there, they are waving at those standing, beckoning them.

The dog stands at the crossing, barking suddenly, but nobody tries to stop him. Maybe he has discovered that the people waiting at the crossing have become empty, soul-less bodies, and he fears those bodies may fall on him anytime. Moving aside quickly, he barks uncontrollably at them, now tilting his head towards them.

All of a sudden, the traffic signal turns red and the vehicles on all sides of the road stop instantly. People waiting here step on the road, carrying on their shoulders the corpses of life itself. Seeing these cadavers crossing the road, the dog barks even more loudly and relentlessly. But no corpse turns to look at him, infuriating him further, until he starts to cross the road after them. Before he knew what he was doing, he reached the other side of the road!

But what is this? This side of the road is the same as the other. The dog feels he has left himself behind on the other side. This is the side of the road he had to cross over to, but he did not reach it at all. Wagging his tail, he reaches the butcher's shop, and the butcher mercilessly throws a big bone at him. Instead of jumping away from it, he jumps towards the bone. Then, screaming helplessly, he runs in the direction of his head. The pain of his injured mouth running faster than him, he stumbles into an elegant young couple. Then he slows down and walks behind them, as if he has suddenly decided to walk with them forever. But where to? Anywhere—or nowhere at all. His wild nostrils sense the smell of friendliness and humanly love, and he forgets the injury in his mouth.

While walking on fondly, somehow, his hind legs shift forward and forelegs fall behind. Men and women walk so close together, it is as if they want to immerse in one another. The dog's heart wants to stand on its hind legs and also climb into the existence of any of these humans. Smelling their love for each other, his restlessness grows, and eyes shut, nostrils flaring, he runs until he overtakes them. He wishes these lovers would include him in their love, so that those who see them say they are not two but three together: two humans and a dog, or no dog, no human, all three are one.

He is excited despite his injury, and hungry and scared that a pedestrian may kick him for no reason. *Don't scold me, people, love me, or at least, don't hate me. I will do all the loving, your part and mine, I will do it all, you have to do nothing. I will do everything to create this relationship between us.* Eager to forge a relationship with this couple, he looks around exuberantly, so that everyone who sees him can share in his joy. The dog is elated that the world will share his love, and starts falling in love with the world—even with the filthy wrestler he has spotted over there.

The wrestler stops ahead of his dairy. He's drinking buttermilk, and twirling his moustache while sitting. It looks as if two dogs sit facing each other in his mouth, their thin tails emerging from each side of his upper lip. Seeing the dog, both dogs in the wrestler's mouth start barking. Before these two dogs can leave the wrestler's mouth and jump on him, the dog runs along the roadside, fleeing for its life. But the two dogs are nowhere to be seen. Nobody knows where they are lost, maybe they crossed the road…

The dog waits at the end of the footpath and looks across to the other side, having forgotten that just a while ago, he had crossed over from that side. He thinks he must go to the other side, that he had always—since the universe began—wanted to cross to that side, but could never make it. He had always stood there, looking this way and that in this life of his, spent along this long road, running in opposite directions. Why should he be on this side but then, equally, why should he cross?

The dog turns his head away from the road. He finds the same couple he had followed near a cloth shop and, trembling with ecstasy, runs towards them. With his teeth, he pulls the woman's sari from behind her. She screams and people run towards her... stones, sticks, kicks, stones. The woman tells her husband he is a mad dog.

'What if he had bitten you, darling?'

'And you know what—last week, this dog bit me in my dream and I died, and, and...'

The husband asks people to beat the dog, thrash him, pulp him to death. 'He is mad, what if he bites someone?'

The woman tells him, 'And you know what, darling? Since last week, wherever I've gone, I've felt this dog is following me. But when I turned, I never saw him. What if, instead of my sari, my ankle had come between his teeth? And darling, just think, what if my sari had come loose in this crowded market? Beat him, the bastard son of a dog!'

The dog is about to collapse, but tries using very human wisdom to find a way to save himself: gathering all his strength, he runs like a bullet, straight ahead, mindlessly, like an animal. A few people chase him, but stop after a bit and go back. The dog runs continuously until he reaches a heap of trash under some trees. He dances with contentment when he smells the trash, and rests his head on the heap, and goes deep into meditation, after ensuring that no one was still chasing him.

The dog continuously scratches the trash heap with his paw, his nose swelling and swelling even more, assuring him that in this heap would be found all objects of use to his belly. His mouth waters like a flowing river and, swimming in his own mouth, he forgets all pain and worry. Kadch, kadch,—trch,—ch! Now the son of a bitch scratches his head—*why does the human species keep its filth out of sight? It is perhaps to remain blind to its own filth*! The dog starts laughing—or barking—kadch,—trch,—ch! These people bathe over and over again, repeatedly cleanse their skin, scrape it incessantly, losing the mark of their identity.

The dog finds a rag and tears into it with his teeth. He finds nothing concealed in the rag. He starts to laugh (or bark) again. If we tear up the clothes of a human, we find sheer emptiness inside. He cannot stop laughing (or barking) at this thought. This morning, he bit a man, but his teeth passed through his pants, and his upper and lower jaws ground against each other.

He had stared at the man then, and wondered—where was his leg? But where was his mind—indeed, the only way to identify man is his clothes. The dog laughs again (or barks?).

Actually, all these thoughts of his sprang from his thought that that beautiful bitch living near the well, who fell in love with him, also dressed like humans. No! She is not so stupid, and even if she were, he would tear her clothes off and throw them away. If, like the humans, I find no evidence of her existence inside her clothes, then I will grind my teeth into her until they are badly wounded, and my wounds will expose her. That's it! In his imagination, the dog starts licking the wounds of his beloved. He starts to like the taste of the blood of the bitch so much that he digs his teeth into her wounds again.

While digging into the heap of trash, he bit the naked arm of a man who lay in the heap, amid all the filth. The man's cry rises from the heap, and the dog runs in the direction from which he had come, the man running after him, screaming: 'Catch him, kill him.' And many people start chasing the dog—'He is mad, a mad dog, kill him, don't let him get away!'

The crowd chasing the dog swells, as the dog runs

towards death while saving himself from death. He runs faster…faster. He reaches the footpath of the same road where he had run away from to save his life.

And on that footpath, someone screams, 'It's him, the mad dog, kill him!'

Desperately, the dog looks back at the people rushing to kill him. He looks helplessly to his right then, and in utter confusion, to his left, from where everyone chasing him was on the verge of reaching him. And then the dog mindlessly leaps onto the busy road of life, as if he had never jumped but vanished in an instant, just as he had stood there. The traffic rushing on the road, life's innumerable vehicles, ran fast, kept running, and the dog's existence could not be seen anywhere. Nobody knows where he is now, on this side, that side, or anywhere.

The Dwellers

(Bashinde)

After almost thirty-six years, I have returned to the city of my birth. The paths that disappeared long ago have filled my dreamy eyes again and, as is their nature, turned towards once familiar destinations. My friend Jamal puts his hand on my shoulder and points towards his car, 'Let's go.' He has come to receive me at the station. Before the creation of Pakistan, Jamal and I used to be roommates in our university hostel. Jamal's home was in Meerut, on the other side of the Pakistan border and mine was in this very city, Sialkot. After the creation of Pakistan, I migrated and settled on the other side of the border, and he moved to Sialkot.

What can one say about plants? They can be uprooted from one place and planted in another. The worst that can happen to them is that they may rot and die if they don't find the environment of their new place favourable. But I have grown so big! Though I was rotting, I was also growing, and as I grew, I hardened and stopped decaying.

A helpless man might not be able to do what his heart desires, but it is his inborn nature to bestow compassion on himself. This, at least, creates within him a fondness for all that he did not like at first but which eventually became a part of him. In this long duration I, too, have gone through this process. My identity and desires are now associated with Delhi. I am obsessed with the fear that if uprooted from there as well, I might turn into ash. Even so, when during a spell of good weather I sway and, seeing me, my innocent branches start swaying too, and their uncountable round leaves cling to the bosom of their branches all at once, in that moment of happiness, I don't know why, I feel the old soil of Sialkot loosening its hold over my roots and instantly, my inner self starts crying, and my spirit revives when this water rains down.

My Sialkot still flourishes in my soul. It has always been my desire to go there once. Even lost dogs and cats, after wandering for a few days, return to their homes far away, wagging their tails. Only humans create such strange rules that has them spend their entire lives aimlessly flying on airplanes, yet failing to cover the distance between themselves and their souls.

'Are you dreaming?' Jamal shakes my shoulder again. 'Come, let's go home.'

I did not recognise him when I got off the train. After such a long and challenging distance in time, where was that bright, young boy? Hidden in the dry white bushes of his beard?

Opening the rear door of the car with one hand, he gently pushes me inside with his other hand. I get in and he enters too, and sits beside me.

'Let's go, driver.' He then shifts his attention towards me.

'Are you still dreaming? Wake up, Mohan!'

I tell him I feel as if I was, indeed, dreaming.

'Open your eyes, friend!' That bushy beard shakes open with laughter and I tiptoe inside to find my hidden friend. He lights a cigarette and passes the pack and a matchbox to me: 'Here—smoke these imported cigarettes.'

'In the desire to collect wealth from all over the world, your India does not import items worth even a rupee!' As I light up, he is reminded of something, and starts laughing boisterously.

'Mohan, do you remember how I would hide your packets of cigarettes? And then we both would turn the room upside down searching for them.' He hits me on my back and guffaws.

'You suspected me, but could do nothing, God forgive me my false oaths.' He continues, 'Ha-ha-ha-ha—we, the believers, were completely ruined in the company of you non-believers!'

He holds and squeezes my hand with both his hands. 'Look there, there—at that alley.' The narrow alley passes by in the blink of an eye and the car surges on. Once, I had brought Jamal to my home from Lahore, and arranged a meeting with Shaeli, who lived in the fifth house on the right side of this very alley.

Shaeli: 'Don't walk next to me, Mohan, walk ahead of me, but listen, not here, a little ahead, or someone might see us. No, I tell you, don't walk next to me, walk behind me.'

Three or four years of my first love were spent running ahead or behind Shaeli and before we could walk together freely, like a couple, she too went across the border and got lost somewhere. Where could I find my interrupted love story on this side of the border? But if thoughts of Shaeli make me almost delirious while I passionately kiss my wife, she looks at me, surprised, wondering how crazy her husband is.

The road in front of our car looks at me and laughs so heartily that multiple potholes form on it and the bumpy ride unsteadies my mind.

'Slow down, driver.'

'Shah-ji, if I drive slowly on this wretched road, the ride will get far bumpier!'

'Fine,' Shah-ji advises his driver, 'But don't drive so fast that the car topples over and we meet with an accident.'

I also used to walk quite fast on this very road, almost blindingly fast. An old and lame Sikh who sold aloo-choley in front of a big electrical goods shop used to stop working whenever he saw me. And, his face concealed behind his bushy white beard, he used to laugh at me. I used to think that he had perceived the love that existed between me and Shaeli, and that he had, in his heart of hearts, created his own story about it. On seeing him, I used to panic and stumble, and stop myself from falling with difficulty. 'Be careful, sir, you have to use your legs your whole life. Walk carefully.'

The many weighty warnings we were given in our younger days—half-forgotten by us now—still dwell in our minds like ghosts waiting for the right opportunity to show themselves. I have no hesitation in accepting that instead of trying to get what I had long pined for, my strategy to protect myself and survive took over, and I put that desire aside. By leading my life so carefully, I have become stable and reliable. But it would have been much better if, like the aloo-choley seller, I, too, had fulfilled some longings of the heart, even at the cost of losing a leg. Then I could have spent my life warning others about taking such risks.

That shop is still there, but someone else runs a hotel there now. No, no, for me, it is still the same—the electric goods shop and the swarms of flies that hover right where that lame man would sit with his paraphernalia. 'Be careful, sir...'

After getting another toss in the car, I control myself from falling, just as I did when I would stumble while walking down this street.

'Driver, slow down,' Jamal instructs the driver again.

The road has learnt about my arrival, and it has run ahead of us, and then looked back at us through the windscreen. 'Mohan, Mohan.' No, it's true, the road is beckoning me! What is so surprising about it? The old road has been here for generations. Even if it is lifeless, it must have come to life by becoming a part of the existence of lakhs of people.

Here in Sialkot, my granny used to tell me, my grandfather passed away in his sleep. The day he was cremated, he stood near the head of Grandmother's bed and woke her up at midnight.

'Nikke's Mother!' (My grandfather used to call my father Nikka.) 'Wake up, Nikke's Mother!' Grandmother told us that she had fallen asleep weeping and dreamt of my grandfather. So, she assumed when she saw him that she was still dreaming and closed her eyes again.

'Get up, oh, Nikke's Ma, get up.'

'Oh, it's you…in the flesh!'

'I thought that since I was unable to meet you before I left, Nikke's Mother, I should return.'

My grandmother told us that the door to her room was wide open.

'Oh, Nikke's Ma, I told the dear old door to open

itself, for that crazy woman must have slept with great difficulty.'

When we asked our grandmother how the door could open by itself, she told us, 'How could it not? Your grandfather himself had got it made.'

Well, isn't that right. What we regard as someone or something's soul has no meaning in itself. Whatever exists acquires meaning only through association. My grandma used to tell us a story about a toymaker. He would take wet clay in his hand and, using his fingertips, transfer his energy into it. So his hands would serve the purpose of a mother's womb, where life originates.

My mother passed away in my childhood but I could visualise her hale and hearty face in the beautiful web of wrinkles on my grandmother's face. Even years later, whenever my sister and I were together, we behaved like our children's children, as if we were still licking the candy and the ghee that granny made whilst we listened to her stories. That is why I cannot stop laughing at my son's idea of a generation gap. How can I make him understand that until my dead grandmother is alive, I will remain my grandchildren's contemporary?

Jamal shakes my shoulder and asks, 'Why are you laughing for no reason?'

'Jamal, I am thinking of my grandmother.'

'Then shed a couple of tears peacefully. Why giggle? Go on, light another cigarette. Your sister-in-law does not even allow me to touch cigarettes, and so I must smoke outside my home.'

We light one more cigarette.

'Mohan, I have not forgotten many of the stories you shared with me, the ones your grandmother told you. The day I received the letter about your arrival, I was reminded of many of those stories.' Jamal gets teary-eyed now. 'It is not good that you have only come here for a day.'

'I have told you that my visa is going to expire.'

'Why did you not come earlier?'

I had already told him that six days were spent doing the task for which I was given my visa.

'You are such a fraud! You have returned after thirty-six years, and that too for just a day!'

After reaching the last street corner, as the driver turns the car to the right, I point to the left and tell Jamal, 'Let us go that way.'

'Yes, let us see your house first.'

No sooner did we turn left from the street corner, all the treasured memories in my heart started reappearing, one after the other.

With Fazle riding piggyback on me, I move from shop to shop in the market, asking: 'Uncle, should the carrier become the one who is carried, or should he continue to carry?'

I threw Fazle down in front of a shop. 'This is enough. No more!'

Fazle reminded me that we cannot end our game before reaching the last shop at the street corner. 'This is my final word!'

Then Fazle caught me by the neck. I punched him. He was stronger than me, and started thrashing me. I started crying. He panicked, 'Oh, don't cry. Come, ride piggyback on me.'

As soon as I climbed on his back, I started smiling through my tears.

Jamal asks me, 'Why are you smiling?'

That night, a big Lohri bonfire was being organised at that crossroads, and the flames were rising so high that people sitting on their terraces across the city felt as if they were all warming themselves at that one bonfire.

And right after crossing the railway tracks there—yes, right there—to the left is Bebe Noora's lane.

'Bebe!'

Invalid and old Bebe, dragging her body on the kutcha floor of her hut, peeped through the door. The wrinkles on her face were stuck on the prickly paths of Kala Pani, where her young son was imprisoned for ages on murder charges. Day and night, poor Bebe wandered around on these very paths, unable to see her immediate surroundings with her poor eyesight.

'Bebe?'

'Who is it?'

'It's me, Mohan, Bebe. *Salam aleykum*, Bebe. Take these jalebis. Grandma has sent them.' Countless blessings started flowing from Bebe's lips. 'May you live long, be prosperous, be happy.'

The fountain of Bebe's blessings falls on the car, leaving me awash with emotion. Jamal asks me, 'Why are you crying?'

Now our car is entering the market on our street. There goes the 'spirit shop' of the naked Chacha.

'Chacha, why don't you wear clothes?'

'Son, naked we came to this world, naked shall we leave!'

Tadaak! As soon as Govind Taya saw me, he hurried down from his sweet shop and, without even asking a question, delivered a tight slap across my face. 'Why do you roam around in the Kanjar Market?' Taya speaks in Urdu when he is angry. Rubbing my cheek, I answered, 'Kanjar Market is on my way to college.' Uncle mellowed down and, giving me two pieces of barfi from his shop, said, '*Lo—khao*!' As soon as I turned after eating the sweets, I heard his advice, 'Go to your college by some other route!'

We have reached our lane. Jamal has asked the driver to stop the car. 'Come, Mohan.'

There's a kind of stillness in the lane. As soon as I step in, I see my grandmother's shadow emerging from the temple in the neighbourhood. After climbing down the stairs, she turns towards the street corner where, towards the left, are the doors to my house. Walking quickly now, I leave Jamal behind. After a while, once she has turned to the left, I glimpse Grandmother's face. I want to walk faster and catch up with her, but when I reach the spot, I find no one there.

I approach my house and stand at my door. The door to my house is closed. I turn my gaze towards the other houses in the neighbourhood. They are lined up next to each other. We used to reach each other's houses through connecting doors. They were all like our own house! The doors to the outside are never used to go from one part of the same house to another.

I knock at the door and a strange thought comes to my mind. It is as if I am somebody else, an outsider, and the one who will open the door from inside will also be my own self—the self I was in the past—a young man. The door will open, and how would I not recognise myself from my past, but he will look at me and enquire: *Who are you*? No, it is not his fault. He has never met me; how would he recognise me?

But the door remains closed. I knock again and wait for an answer. Meanwhile, I notice that both the outer windows are also shut. No sooner do I lift my hands to knock again, I stop, hearing the voice of an unknown woman, 'The owners are not home.'

Jamal's hand is on my shoulder with sorrowful softness. 'Let's go, Mohan.'

With slow and silent steps, we leave the lane and sit in our car.

'Let's go, driver,' Jamal turns away from the driver and looks at me. 'Want to smoke?'

Without waiting for my answer, he lights two

cigarettes and passes one to me. With long drags, we both silently fill our minds with so much smoke that we can no longer think straight.

Our car speeds down the open road of the bridge over the Bhed. Jamal breaks his silence and tells me that he lives in the same locality.

'There used to be a Krishna temple here?'

'Arrey, yes, that temple is my home now.'

I find it very strange that humans dwelled in God's house now.

'Finally! We have reached.'

My mind cannot rid itself of the image of the old temple and cannot see any changes Jamal has made to the structure of the temple in order to live in it. When we enter from the gate, Jamal's family gets up from the lawn and walks towards us. After we alight from the car, Jamal introduces his wife to me: 'Meet my wife.' '*Salam aleykum,*' she says, addressing me. '*Walaikum as-salam,* Bhabhi.' Her flawless greeting makes me feel a little ashamed of my alien manners.

'Did you hear that, Begum?' Jamal of Uttar Pradesh says. 'Such perfect enunciation by my pal! Merely three-four years of my company turned this Punjabi into a civilised human being, while you, even after spending your entire life with me, remain a Punjaban.'

'So what?' his wife answers. 'Urdu is not all I know, but you, what do you know besides Urdu?'

'That remark is a result of your closed mind, Begum,' Jamal then turns his attention to me. 'Do you remember, Mohan? You would speak in such an uncouth dialect and I warned you that if you don't speak Urdu properly, I would change my hostel room. But how can I do that with my wife?'

We all started laughing. 'Mohan, this is my daughter-in-law, and this is my daughter. Her husband is an engineer in Saudi Arabia and here is my son…'

Seeing the boy, it is as if the same old Jamal has resurfaced from my memories and come to life. *Give it back, give it back to me, that's my pack of cigarettes.*

The thought has brought a smile on my face but I am sad because the little boy cannot see me the way I see him. Had my son been here instead of me, then old Jamal and old Mohan would have been meeting in the present moment.

'Mohan is leaving tomorrow,' Jamal tells his wife, 'It's good for us. Don't we have other things to do?'

'Friend, why are you getting angry?'

'Feed this baniya such good food, Begum, that he savours its taste even in his dal-rice.'

'Driver!' Then he looked around.

'Yes Shali-ji! Yes.'

'Keep his luggage in my bedroom.' Then he looks at me and says, 'Though let there be one night of blessing—we shall spend this night as roommates once more. Begum, just for today, please don't stop me from smoking. Take this, Mohan, smoke.'

He passes one cigarette and tips another between his lips. 'You can go with the driver, Mohan. Freshen up, and then we will sit together.'

While climbing the stairs of the temple with the driver, moments from the past came rushing back before my eyes, of when I would come here every Janmashtami to take prasad. Every Janmashtami, Krishna would take birth at night and, completing his lifespan in exactly one year, the God would be reborn again, exactly at the same time the following year. These days, I might not celebrate any other festival, but I celebrate Janmashtami enthusiastically and with fervour as I sing and rock the god in his cradle. His childhood and helplessness evoke my maternal instinct, and I have an intense desire to save him from the fires of Kaliyuga.

Passing through the corridor, we come to a hall

and next to it is Jamal's bedroom, where the driver keeps my luggage to one side. He indicates where the bathroom is and tells me, 'You may wash up, sir.'

As soon as he leaves the room, I pull comfortable clothes out of my suitcase and go to the bathroom. After washing my hands and face, as I wipe my face with a towel, suddenly, I see a cockroach in the washbasin. For some reason, I smilingly convey my greetings to him, '*Salam aleykum,*' and then again, correcting myself on being reminded of Jamal, '*As-salam aleykum.*' The cockroach flutters his wings in reply, '*Walaikum as-salam.*' And then it disappears from sight. When I return to the hall after changing, I find Jamal waiting for me. I sink into the sofa near him and ask him to take out his pack of imported cigarettes. While handing over the pack to me, he tells me, 'Krishna's idol was kept in this room... there... near the window.'

'Yes, I know.' I continuously stare at the window.

'Arrey!' He jumps off the sofa all of a sudden. 'It's time for my namaz... I'll be back.'

He stands and leaves through the door, and I come and stand near that window. By looking at the traces of cement marks at the centre of the window, it can be inferred that the idol had been here. I continuously stare in its direction and, after looking at it steadily for a while, I suddenly hear the ringing of bells in my mind. And Krishna Bhagwan emerges out of my eyes, goes straight to his place, and stands there.

'*Bol Krishna Bhagwan ki Jai.*' (Say 'Glory to Krishna Bhagwan.') The whole hall echoes with the praises coming from the countless people seated there. 'Bhagwan Krishna has taken birth! Take this prasad! Eat it.' My grandmother has stuffed my mouth with so many sweets that I cannot speak, but in my heart, I sing along with the others, '*Bol Krishna Bhagwan ki Jai.*'

Krishna Bhagwan became an adult as soon as he was born, holding the flute to his lips, the butter-smooth gopis dancing on the sweet melody from the dusky Krishna's flute...While dancing, the gopis get delirious...All they want is to remain in this trance forever. They want to dance forever and ever. The sangat that sat in the hall joined the pandit in singing 'Radhe-Shyam, Radhe-Shyam, Radhe'. Krishna Bhagwan has left Vrindavan, but Radha keeps dancing, as if Krishna with his flute to his lips is still playing his tune.

'No, please, don't stop poor Radha! Don't tell her that an era has passed since Bhagwan has left.' Sounds of the hiccups of sobs can be heard in the hall. 'Let Radha dance, don't stop her.' The sounds of hiccupping and sobbing grow louder. I turn my face towards the sound and find the hall empty; there's nobody except Bhagwan and I. I turn my attention towards Bhagwan again. Bhagwan is standing there. No, no, not there, he is resting his back against the wall and he has neither the flute nor the Sudarshan Chakra in his hand. His head is crownless and his arms dangle by his sides.

I pity the loneliness of Bhagwan.

'Bhagwan!' I open my mouth to console him.

Suddenly, Bhagwan jumps and stands straight. 'Arrey, the time for namaz is running out.'

Blinking my eyes, when I look again, he has left.

Rivers of Thirst

(Daryaon Pyas)

Bebe is alone, sitting on a charpai in the verandah of her only son's new bungalow, lost in thought. The wrinkles on her face, heavy with the weight of past events, have sunk into the legs of the charpai and it seems as if the old wooden legs will collapse at their wrinkles.

Bebe lifts her head and looks into the distance but sees nothing. She is not blind, yet what can she do if scenes from her past cover her eyes like a heavy curtain? Memories of their old, ancestral haveli, where countless rooms open one after another and…and… Bebe smiles faintly when, at that very moment, her stretched wrinkles return to the shores of her face from the legs of the charpai, revealing her fully in her own features.

Her husband is going crazy, searching for her in one room and the next, while she sits in this verandah, involuntarily laughing loudly. Her husband, chasing her tinkling silvery laughter, enters the room and gathers her tightly in his arms.

At this moment, the entire picture of the haveli is etched on Bebe's face, and her laughter runs around, chiming from one room to another. Her charpai creaks, striving to make her comprehend: Bebe! Think of your age. People already call you crazy. But Bebe wouldn't listen to the charpai at that moment, for only her body lay on it.

'I got worried! Where did you wander off to?'

'Even if I were lost, I would be somewhere in these very rooms,' she laughs and tells her husband. 'Even when I die, I will remain in these rooms. Look, if you cannot find me in any of the open rooms after I die, here, a bunch of keys to the haveli is tied to my saree pallu, and you might find me asleep in another room, tired after waiting for you.'

Bebe is restless and half-reclines on the bed, pulling the edge of her dupatta towards her chest, holding a huge bunch of keys in her hand. The constant gentle rubbing of her fingers against the metal of these keys for fifty to fifty-five years has made the metal smooth as flesh, and from the body of every key, its soul seems to peep out.

One key opens the kitchen.

'Many times have I told you to be on time, at least for meals, but who listens to me? You're here at last? Wait, I'm coming!'

'And *this* key? My Munna uses this room to study. Haven't I told you already—see the lamp burning by his head. Your Munna is fast asleep, holding the book in his hands. You nag the poor boy for no reason. Who knows, he might be studying in his dreams too.'

'Bebe, I am the father of a child, but you treat me like a child. You should call me by my name.'

'When I think of calling you by your name, I feel as if I am calling my daughter-in-law's husband, not my own son…'

'Then you should address me as the husband of your daughter-in-law, Bebe. How can I remain your Munna all my life?'

Bebe's trembling fingers let go of the key to Munna's study and began touching the key to the room where her husband worked.

'Come, Munna's Bebe, come, why have you stopped? Arrey, why are you weeping? Tell me—I'll make everything alright. Give me all your sorrow. Why should you weep when I am here?'

'This is, in fact, the reason for my weeping—that you are no longer around. Me? I would have stayed to take care of you even after I died…'

Bebe starts weeping quietly but if her tears had not flowed, it would have been impossible to tell that she was crying from her dry, shrivelled, wrinkle-ridden, misshapen face.

A key has sprung into her hand all by itself, and now the door to the room it opens is ajar, and people are taking away the corpse of her husband.

'No! No! Let him walk on his own. If he goes on his own, he always finds his way back home. If you take him away, he will never return. No, don't take him away. I have lived my whole life in this haveli. I know nothing about the world beyond its walls. How will I find him?'

People whisper, Bebe has gone mad.

'Yes, I have gone mad. Let me go mad, otherwise I will really go mad…'

The monsoon has descended on Bebe's eyes though

the weather is so dry outside that a tree beside the lawn facing the verandah whispers to another tree: 'Look, the shower of rain from the old woman's eyes is being wasted on the floor.' 'Yes, if it were to fall on the earth around us, it would nourish us.'

Holding the bunch of keys in her hands, Bebe appears to hold her entire old haveli to her chest.

Standing before her dying husband, Bebe wept.

'Don't cry, you crazy woman. I have very little time left.'

Trying to muffle the sound of her weeping, she gagged her mouth with her dupatta.

'Don't cry, and listen to me. Stay in this haveli till your last breath. That's also my advice to Munna; that till he passes his law exam, he should live here. His wedding must be celebrated with great pomp—are you listening? We have been living in this haveli for several generations. Our fathers and grandfathers gather here at every wedding or death. On my wedding, I saw them all with my eyes; even my dead father was among them. And others, too, were there. Do you hear me? If you stay here, you will always be with me. Do not leave this haveli on any condition, or else we will be separated forever. Look, here they come, my father, my grandfather, his father... all of them.'

Bebe has really gone mad. The poor thing has no idea if she is in her home or if she lost that home years ago in order to come here. The day is still preserved undamaged in her mind when they locked the entire haveli and walked out and her dead husband, father-in-law, and many generations of other members of her husband's family came to the door to see them off.

Her husband's ghost stepped forward and tapped her shoulder.

'Go, Munna's Bebe. Things have worsened here. It is best that you leave, or else they will shed your blood. No, do not worry about us, we don't have any blood, so how could it flow? But you must return as soon as things are better. Lock the outside door. We will be waiting for you and pass the time counting every moment...'

'No, you forbade me from stepping out of the haveli, and now you are turning me out?'

'No, Munna's Bebe, God forbid! Should somebody murder you, I would have to pursue him even to hell, and I won't be able to return from there.'

'No!'

'No, Munna's Bebe, you must leave for now. Wherever you might go, this place will be your real destination. Go wherever you can now, or we will have to be apart forever.'

A glut of pain opened in Madre Hind's womb, and as soon as she gave birth to her blood-soaked twins, she breathed her last, unleashing a calamity. Someone! Please bathe these motherless innocents, cover them with soft and warm clothing, think of their comfort and their food. But who cares when doomsday hovers overhead? Mobs are attacking each other and the sight of severed human limbs has become so commonplace that only in the form of a ghost can the completeness of a human being be imagined.

It is in these times that these two aged ghosts, one of a living woman and the other of her dead husband, are parting from each other. Bebe touches the bunch of keys tied to her pallu, and as she turns her back to the haveli, she clearly hears:

'Don't worry, Munna's Bebe, you are leaving only to return.'

~

'Let's go, Bebe.' Her grown-up son, a lawyer, extends his hand to support her.

'No! No!' Bebe pulls back her extended hand. 'This haveli is all the support I have.'

She sprints back to the door of her haveli and the key thrusts its body into the lock and opens it.

'No, Munna's Bebe!'

Her dead husband is still standing inside the doorway: 'Go!'

'No!'

'No—go away!'

Crazed Bebe has suddenly become silent, following her son as if she doesn't know where she is going. Deep within herself, through dried up arteries, she stumbles along on this journey to her existence, and she's still there—where she always has been—here in this haveli.

Outside the haveli, it is a powder keg; fires everywhere, explosions everywhere, but the inside of the haveli is so safe, so peaceful, and bustling.

Bebe's ability to speak revives.

'Didn't I tell you, Munna's Bebe, wherever you may go, on your own you will return here.'

'Yes! Go and rest. I have to warm the milk for Munna. It's time for him to return from the courts.'

'Bebe! Bebe! How should I tell you? You are driving me crazy too.'

'May your enemies be crazy, Munna, I am here to go mad for you.'

'You certainly are, Bebe. How can I explain to you that we have left our haveli, our town, our land across the border... We left many years ago, but you seem to be living right there even today.'

'Where else can I live, Munna? You can go to live and prosper anywhere, but all I have is this haveli of my ancestors.'

Bebe rubs the tips of her fingers lovingly over the bunch of keys to the haveli.

'Even a mad person cannot be this mad, Bebe. You still roam around with the keys to the haveli tied to your pallu.'

'Drink your milk, Munna.'

'What good will milk do me, Bebe? I wish I could turn these keys in such a way as to somehow, just once, unlock you. Do you know that no girl is ready to marry me because of your madness?'

'Do you hear? Come out of your room. Look, our Munna has brought his bride. What kind of a father are you? There are wedding celebrations and music playing in your haveli. I don't think even death can turn a person this deaf. Come outside! Come, bahu, I will take you to your father-in-law. Poor thing, he died wondering when his son would become a lawyer and when he would bring home his bride. Come, daughter-in-law, he must be sitting lost in that room, busy with his official papers. As soon as he sees you, he will cheer up and forget all about his work. Come. Daughter-in-law! Daughter-in-law! Daughter-in-law! Spend a little time with me too. I wish you'd talk to me.'

'Bebe, what can one talk about with mad people?'

'No, Munna, I am not mad. I am not, Munna. Call me by my full name.'

'What is your full name? Dear, are you listening? What is the full name of our Munna? Daughter-in-law! Daughter-in-law. You are pregnant. Now you must stop working!'

'If I stop working, what will we eat, Bebe?'

'Why should we worry about food, daughter-in-law? Our haveli is loaded with stores of grain. Come, let me unlock the rooms and show you.'

'Bebe! You will drive the entire household crazy. If not about me, at least think about your daughter-in-law.'

'Who can compare with my daughter-in-law? Dear, are you listening? Look, your daughter-in-law has given birth to our grandson. Look, his forehead is like our Munna's. Look here, his chin, too, is like Munna's.

Dear, are you listening? What kind of a grandfather are you? You don't even step out of your room. Look at who has come to our haveli...'

'Don't make a noise Bebe, let your daughter-in-law rest.'

'But Munna, I only...'

'I have told you so many times, Bebe, I am not your little Munna anymore.'

'If you are not Munna, then whose mother am I?'

'The way you are troubling us with your madness now makes me suspicious that you are not my mother.'

'Dear, are you listening? Come out of your dark room and listen to what your Munna is telling me.'

Bebe tosses restlessly on the charpai in the verandah outside her son's new bungalow and the charpai is creaking and speaking to her.

'Go to sleep, Bebe, why don't you sleep comfortably?'

'Yes, I know I must go to sleep.'

Bebe has closed her eyes and has started thinking that her son, daughter-in-law, and grandson have been out for too long and not returned. They must be about to return. Yes, they are coming back.

'Bebe! Oh! Look. Bebe has... Bebe has... Bebe...'

Her Munna has started to weep and so have her daughter-in-law and her grandson.

'No, little one, you must not weep,' Bebe instantly opens her eyes and stretches her arms towards him, but seeing no one there, she closes her eyes again and assumes that she is dead. Now, the madwoman feels that she is really mad because how can one be dead by just closing one's eyes?

'Water!'

The walls of the verandah answer: 'If you are thirsty, you must help yourself Bebe, what can we do?'

Bebe gets up from the bed with great difficulty and from the table close by, attempts to pick up the jug in her trembling hands, but the empty jug slips from her hands. It falls on to the floor and makes a loud clanging noise like her hot-tempered son.

Frightened, she sits on the charpai.

'Look what we have brought for you, Bebe.'

'What have you brought, little one?'

On hearing her grandson's voice, she immediately turns around.

But there is no one there.

Her thirst has grown.

With parched eyes, she stares at the door that

connects the verandah to the interior of the bungalow, on which her son and daughter-in-law have put a lock.

'Look, his entire forehead is like our Munna's. Look at this, his chin is also…'

'Dear, are you listening?'

'Yes, I am listening, Munna's Bebe, but whom are you talking about? This is our Munna. Oh! Yes, this is our Munna!'

'Come inside, Munna's Bebe, why are you sitting outside? But you must veil your face. Your father-in-law is coming this way. No, he has left. Oh! Come now, open the lock and come without any hesitation. Come. Come, have some water and give me some too. *Come*!'

Bebe has suddenly gained energy from God alone knows where, and she quickly heads for the locked door which leads to the inside of the bungalow. She stands before it and begins turning each of the keys to the haveli into the lock one by one, but the lock just does not open.

Three Short Stories

(Teen Afsanche)

Kargil

(Kargil)

Abdul spotted two dead bodies lying in the opening between the hills, and tiptoed towards them. One was a Hindustani soldier, and the other a Pakistani mujahid. Both their rifles lay fallen on the ground that stretched between them. But what business did Abdul have with guns? If he were caught carrying the guns, the army would have taken him for a mujahid and nabbed him!

Everyone had fled the village, but Abdul had taken refuge in some hidden cave in the hills. And on every such opportunity, he would rummage through the pockets of corpses for anything useful and, thanking Allah, secure it in his own pocket.

In the mujahid's inner pocket, he found a letter in the handwriting of a child. The image of the small note with a child's words playing hopscotch on paper made him smile, and he began reading, 'Dear Abbu, *As-salam aleykum*. Yesterday was my birthday, but who knows where you've gone. That's why Ammi and I wept all day long'.

Abdul shivered in the gusts of the icy winds, and found his attention shifting to the pockets of the Hindustani soldier. In the soldier's outer pocket, he found a photograph of an utterly beautiful little girl.

The simple-hearted thief was stunned: how did the photograph of the mujahid's daughter get into the pocket of the Hindustani soldier?

The House of God
(Khana-e-Khuda)

My old mother used to live with my brother before she came to stay with me. As the gurudwara was right next to my brother's house, after bathing and before breakfast, my mother used to visit it regularly to pay obeisance. But I lived in a Muslim locality in Delhi and there was no gurudwara in the vicinity. For a few days, before going to the office, I took her in my car to a distant gurudwara. Then, on hearing about the usual delay in reaching my office on those days, she said, 'Son, you don't have to take this trouble'.

'Then how will you go to see your Waheguru, Ma?'

My old and innocent mother thought for a while and came up with a solution, 'I will go to the nearby masjid and bow my head for the Waheguru there.'

War, Jihad, Et Cetera Et Cetera (Jung, Jihad, Vagairah, Vagairah)

First the two countries kept threatening each other, and in that atmosphere of fear and suspicion, they got so frustrated that they both launched hydrogen bomb-enabled missiles at each other.

And then, in a feverish haste, lakhs of souls, creating a lot of chaos, wailing and screaming, gathered near the gates of hell. The angels appealed to God: 'O Lord of the two worlds! Where is the space in hell for so many souls?'

The order was passed by God: take as many as fit into the space.

'But what about the remaining people?'

'Send the rest back so that they can live in their own hell.'

Sleepwalkers

(Khwabrau)

1

This is Lucknow.

The minute the Partition refugees from Lucknow found their feet in Karachi, they erected that same square in Ameenabad here as well. Here, too, those very same six-seven streets with tilted caps angled their way into the square from here and there, and it looked as if the whole world was headed this way. Soon, there wasn't a single square inch of space left in Ameenabad, and the refugees started settling down all around it.

Just like that, bit by bit, all of Lucknow got settled in Karachi. Not just the old city, but a brand new town sprang from the old one and began spreading its own special sparkle everywhere. They say people come and go, places stay put, but here, the refugees had carried the entire city intact in their hearts—some the bricks of their house, some the whole house, some brought their entire street, some the big busy road right behind the street—whatever they could fit into their hearts, they brought…and when they were finally able to catch their breath in Karachi, brick by brick, they plucked the whole city out from their hearts. God alone knows what is left where this city used to be. But here, it is burgeoning so uninhibitedly that when someone returns from Karachi, they're constantly asked, 'Did you see the Lucknow in Karachi?'

Late at night, when the colourful lights would begin their eerie dance on the quiet roads of Ameenabad, the people sleeping in the pitch dark of their homes would still be circling around the crowded square in their dreams. In the beginning, Manva Chowkidaar would thump his thick cane on the road to ward off the jitters and just stare at the dazzling lights in disbelief—the whole square is empty, then who in Allah's name do I keep bumping into? Even more puzzling was that, in just a few more days, he really began seeing all those people's shadows. And then it happened that while Manva Chowkidar was unable to see crooks and thieves, he saw all those who had walked, in their dreams, into the square.

'Arrey Bhaiyya, why are you all clambering all over me?'

That night, Manva Chowkidar bumped into someone first and then leapt back, but it dawned upon him that this was our very own Deewane[3] Maulvi Sahab. Very respectfully, he called out, '*Salam aleikum,* Maulvi Sahab.'

'*Walaikum as-salam,* Manva,' Deewane Maulvi Sahab pulled out a two-rupee note from his pocket and crushed it into Manva Chowdikar's palm. 'Thank you, Maulvi Sahab, may Allah always grant us your blessings.' Manva Chowkidar was barely done smacking his fingertips and saying 'Ameen' than Deewane Maulvi Sahab was already gone.

'But how is this possible, Manva Chacha?' Ajijo the chaiwallah asked, extending the teacup towards Manva Chowkidar.

'But brother, if it's not possible, where did this two-rupee note come from?' Manva took out the new two-rupee note and showed it to him.

'Who knows, maybe it was a ghost or a spectre?'

'So what if it was a ghost or an apparition? It's still our Deewane Maulvi Sahab,' Manva Chowkidar paused a little to draw a sip of his tea. 'Forget others, Ajijo, I even saw you walking towards the market.'

'But I was happily in slumberland at that time, Chacha!'

'Yes, that's exactly what happens. Everyone comes out on the streets while fast asleep at home.'

'Your claptrap is beyond my grasp, Chacha! If people are actually out in the streets at night, I would keep my tea stall open all night as well!'

'Deewane Maulvi Sahab can be seen very clearly in the crowd every day, Ajijo!'

'Such tall tales you tell, Chacha!'

Deewane Maulvi Sahab's actual name is Nawab Mirza Kamaluddin, but he is known by everyone as Deewane Maulvi Sahab, and he has gotten so accustomed to this name that if someone calls him Nawab Kamaluddin, he thinks the poor fellow has mistaken him for someone else. The other refugees have, of their own accord, established a new Lucknow in Karachi, but Deewane Maulvi Sahab thinks he is still living in the same old Lucknow. Initially, many friends tried to explain to him that he has come away from there, but even in the old Lucknow, it was his habit that whenever he went out of the city, he would be restless until he returned. Wherever he went, it was always from Lucknow to Lucknow.

His wife, Acchi Begum, says that they had just barely arrived in Karachi when Deewane Maulvi Sahab began his refrain of 'Let's go back to Lucknow'. And if some well-meaning soul ever asked, 'What, after all, remains in Lucknow now,' he would shoot back: 'Lucknow!'

'Here, look at this nonsense!' Acchi Begum continues her commentary, 'Our children are here, relatives are here, friends and acquaintances are here. What's left there now? Only Lucknow is left in Lucknow. So why would we go there now—to swat flies? But who could reason with Deewane Maulvi Sahab? He wanted to go there precisely because only Lucknow contains his Lucknow, and wherever Lucknow is, there he is.'

'So did you manage to keep our Maulvi Sahab here in Karachi?'

'If your Deewane Maulvi Sahab ever heeded me, would anyone call him deewana?' It was his Acchi Begum who had given Deewane Maulvi Sahab this name. That is why even hearing it from strangers made them seem like near and dear ones to him. 'But that's all said and done now, bhai, we never went back to Lucknow; Lucknow itself came here.'

'Lucknow itself came here?'

'Yes, what else? It had already burnt to ashes, and whatever was left of it followed us here. What a poor little thing it had become! Not a hair more than the smallest little bit of Ameenabad. Deewane Maulvi Sahab ran to embrace it and sobbed inconsolably.'

'And then, Begum Sahiba?'

'All of Lucknow knows the rest of the tale. By and by, this ramshackle Ameenabad began to blossom again. First, a stem sprouted, then that branch, and then each and every one of them; and like that, our Lucknow came back to life as-is. In fact, more beautiful than it ever had been.'

'So did our Deewane Maulvi Sahab stop asking to go back then?'

'Only the mad understand the mad! Such were things that if ever we said, "Please go, get your visa made, let's go pray on the graves of our ancestors," he would fire back with, "Have you sent your brains on a furlough? According to you, are our ancestors' graves somewhere abroad? Arrey bhai, if you want to say prayers on their graves, let's go do it right away!" If I seemed confused, he'd say more gently, "My Acchi Begum, after all, how far is our family graveyard? Two lanes away on the hump of Nazeerabad is Chhote Mamu's tomb, and from here to the right, just a little further, just a stone's throw away, there's our ancestral graveyard." Then I would plead with him, "I don't feel well, Deewane Maulvi Sahib! I don't want to go today." But he would stay adamant, "May our enemies be foiled by illnesses; so what if you're not feeling well? After all, shirking your pious responsibility is no less than a sin."'

Acchi Begum also tells of how Deewane Maulvi Sahab believes all of Lucknow to be mad—'What strange times these are! Even in one's own city, one feels that one is getting stifled in a foreign land.'

'Arrey Mian!' he would go to houses near and far to explain again and again, 'Turn to Allah and read all five namaaz with all your heart. What bigger pain is there than when, sitting in your own house, you feel you're not at home.'

'But Maulvi Sahib ...'

'No, Mian, these ifs and buts won't work. When the

whole town suffers from the same malaise, then it's a serious matter. Who knows, maybe this is Allah's wrath upon this town for our collective sins.'

'But listen, Maulvi Sahib …'

'What should I listen to, Mian? You listen to me, and turn to Allah at once.'

The old residents of Karachi's Lucknow would even find some truth in the senile commentary of Deewane Maulvi Sahib. They'd think that if it's not Allah's wrath, why do they feel this way? Despite recreating Lucknow brick for brick, why did they feel like strangers in their own homes?

It was not as if the mohajirs had not made any economic progress as refugees. In fact, in some respects, they had surpassed not only the Sindhis, but local Pakistanis. With their hard work and ingenuity, they dominated in business, industry, and bureaucracy at both the state and national levels. In fact, it's as if Lucknow's streets had opened up and expanded in and around Karachi to reach Meerut, Moradabad, Malihabad, Azamgarh, or Allahabad much faster. Four or five years ago, when his cousin came to visit Deewane Maulvi Sahab from India's Lucknow, he began losing his mind in shock. 'What can I say,

Mr Maulvi Sahib? I am beginning to feel that this is the real Lucknow. That it's not you but we who perhaps migrated from here to there.'

The cousin turned towards Deewane Maulvi, expecting praise for his observation. 'We haven't moved from anywhere to anywhere, Bhai,' Deewane Maulvi Sahib said, wondering if he had run into another lunatic, 'Its tourists like you who come and go. And listen, one place cannot be at two places the same time. Our Lucknow is the only Lucknow. We don't consider any other place Lucknow—understood?' He extended his silver case that held a special paan made with crushed saffron-infused tobacco leaves towards his guest, 'And listen, maybe you'll be shocked to hear this, brother, but you cannot belie the truth. Local people are rooted in their place. If you don't believe me, should I open my mouth and show you?—Look—my dear sir, come closer and look inside my throat. A whole soiree of Nawab Asifuddaulah's thumris is in full swing. Hahaha!'

2

For the mohajirs in Karachi, the issue is that despite being denizens of Karachi, they were forced to remain refugees here. One or two from amongst them lost their marbles and went mad with shock, but even those who didn't lose them all are utterly puzzled about how to tune Nawab Asifuddaulah's thumri to Sai Bulleshah's kafi on the chimta. Whatever it is, these two distinct notes will only harmonise if there is a genuine attempt to synchronise them. No matter how melodic the sarangi and the chimta might be, their disparate sounds would only produce a grating cacophony if not carefully blended.

Initially, their pandemonium was drowned out in the chaos of the independence and partition of India, but once the widespread chaos subsided, the rule of the guard and the police began to return, and the refugees began to find their feet. Once again, you could clearly hear the disharmonious notes. In the initial years, things had come to such a pass that all you heard was the deafening sounds of the riots between the locals and the mohajirs. And wherever it was quiet, you knew that some big explosion could blow out your eardrums any moment.

The nawabs of Lucknow, whether they're actual nawabs or just in name, are nevertheless habitually aristocratic. So patient and steadfast that even if you send them up some long winding path and take the shortcut yourself, they would still have arrived at the destination before you, and completed their coronation ceremony. Then, even if you came charging at them with a grenade in hand, the minute you got close, you'd go limp, enchanted by their charming smiles. With tremendous calm, they'll take the grenade out of your fist, tuck it away in some corner, and invite you to talk about reconciliation and friendship, as if that's what you came there for.

'But it takes two hands to clap, Chando.' Deewane Maulvi Sahab's son Nawab Mirza would lovingly call his wife, Chand Bibi, 'Chando'. He is the general secretary of the Anjuman-e-Ahliyan-e-Lucknow and the proprietor of a big shoe factory that employs at least one hundred Sindhis, a few Pathans, and one Punjabi craftsmen. 'The Opposition needs to act with self-restraint too, doesn't it,' he says as he stretches out on his bed, 'Now take my own workmen, for example. Except for perhaps five or six of them, the rest are all lazy and inept. And, God forbid, if I so much as threaten to dismiss any of them, they all go on strike without any notice.'

'You shouldn't bother picking arguments with

them,' Chand Bibi offers him some wise words, 'The work still gets done after all.'

'What do you mean "it gets done"? If I don't even exert this much authority, they'll send me packing. They say, "The factory is as much ours as yours." And not in some proverbial way, Chando—they really mean it. Leave alone the factory; left to them, they won't rest until they've driven Nawab Mirza all the way out of town!'

'Instead of this daily bickering, it'd be better if you shut down the factory.'

'Shut it down and go where? We, too, have helped build Pakistan. In fact, we are the ones who made it.'

Seeing her husband distraught like this, Chand Bibi sits by his pillow and runs her fingers through his hair.

'Whatever argument one might offer, Chando, they only have one stock response: that they are locals.'

'Look, you go off to Pakistan every morning.' (Nawab Mirza's factory is some distance away from Lucknow and its satellite refugee towns, in a Sindhi neighbourhood.) 'God forbid, what if something goes wrong?'

'Don't you worry about me, Chando! No matter where I am, I am forever at home.'

'Haha! Hahaha!' Nawab Mirza's lawyer brother Ishaq Mirza can never resist laughing at his older brother's tales.

Ishaq Mirza was born in Karachi and even finished his studies here. After completing his Masters' degree in law from Karachi University, despite strict opposition from his family members, he married a Sindhi girl. From then on, he exiled himself from Lucknow and began living in an old Sindhi neighbourhood with his family. For over two years after his wedding, he didn't so much as see his own people. Then we got news that separation from him was giving Acchi Begum fainting spells, so he started visiting Lucknow. And now he's made it a habit to bring his wife and children here every Thursday afternoon, and return only after dinner.

Seeing Ishaq Mirza laughing at his words, Nawab Mirza gets irritated.

'What's there to be annoyed about, Bhai jaan?' Ishaq never lets go of any opportunity to state his opinion, 'Us Lucknow-wallahs—I mean *you* Lucknow-wallahs—because, you see, I'm from right here, Karachi—your problem is exactly this that you never leave your home.'

'What nonsense are you muttering, Ishaq?' Why

would his sister-in-law Chand Bibi ever let go the opportunity to interrupt him? 'My poor husband spends his entire day outside the house. It's such a relief when he returns home in the evening, safe and sound. I don't understand why your in-laws' community is after our lives. They want to flush us all out!'

'There's no water in those old neighbourhoods' taps, Chand Bibi.' His brother and sister-in-law could not stand this habit of Ishaq's, of spitting words out of his mouth, 'Why would those people spare the water to flush you out? All they want is for you all to live in fellowship with them.'

'Nah, brother!' His sister-in-law's bubbly and spirited repartee amuses Ishaq no end, 'After all, we've already sacrificed you for fellowship with them.'

'Look, Bhabhi—and Bhaijaan, you must think too—is it right that we buy up their lands and homes with their own money, and then establish our Lucknows and Malihabads here?' Right beside Lucknow, in Malihabad, the two brothers' uncle, Hakim Jalamuddin, has erected a massive mansion. Ishaq still has his mouth open to continue his exposition, but his brother stops him, 'Wait! Stop this nonsense! What is this absurd point you're raising about us buying with their money…'

'The point has already arisen, Bhaijaan, now you can pontificate about the theoretical details yourself. What I have understood, broadly, is that a Muslim's earnings are meant for anyone in need. Not only that, it is a Muslim's duty that wherever he is fated to live, he should live there like a native.

'You are absolutely right, Qibla Maulvi Sahab!' Nawab Mirza could not let go of a single opportunity to be sarcastic, 'But so profusely does your preaching rain down on this house that it is making our whole house drip, and yet your near and dear ones remain parched. Why have you kept them deprived of your benefactions?'

Often, Deewane Maulvi Sahab would suddenly appear when they were in the middle of their arguments. Last time too, when both brothers had drawn their swords, Deewane Maulvi Sahab was spotted right then, walking in from somewhere outside into the drawing room.

'Aha! Khushamdeed! Welcome, Chhote Nawab Sahab!' Deewane Maulvi was perhaps debating whether to sit with them or go deposit the things he bought at the market with his wife.

'*As-salam aleykum*, Abba jaan!'

'*Walaikum as-salam*, beta, all along the way, I kept thinking I had forgotten something. Seeing you has reminded me that today's the day you visit Lucknow.'

'That is why I am here, Abba jaan!'

'Bhai Ishaq, at any rate, you are very unfortunate. Even though you belong to Lucknow, you're living thousands of miles away in Karachi.'

Like always, Ishaq smiles in response.

'Look at this!' Maulvi Sahab takes out a giant ripe mango from his sling bag and offers it to Ishaq Mirza, 'Here, have it. It's an authentic Malihabadi mango.'

Ishaq Mirza's mouth savours the taste of mango, but the moment he takes it in his hands his face falls, 'But this is clay!'

'It's an authentic Malihabadi!' Deewane Maulvi Sahab begins to laugh, 'I've brought it from the guy who makes clay fruits at the sandal market.' Deewane Maulvi Sahab decides he might as well go in and give the shopping bags to his wife after all, 'I'll be right back.'

'Here, Bhaijaan, taste this Malihabadi mango', seeing Deewane Maulvi Sahab turn around to walk away, Ishaq says, 'Let's see you eat it. Your whole mouth will be filled with nothing but clay.'

'Arre, Chhote bhai, who needs to eat the mango? We are satiated just looking at it.'

'No, Bhaijaan, there's no surviving without feeding the belly. Don't you find it absurd? We eat mangoes grown right here, but our hearts are only appeased by the clay mangoes of Malihabad.'

'That is what is culture, Ishaq Mian! What would you know about the taste of culture?'

Chand Bibi had also quietly come and joined them a short while ago. Bored with their conversations, she stands up.

'Ishaq bhai, Acchi Amma gets very annoyed by your wife's language. They both must be fed up of each other.' Then, after some thought, she suddenly yells, 'Haye Allah! Where are the children? I can't hear any of them!'

'Wherever they are, Bhabhi, let them be,' Ishaaq Mirza lets out a little laugh watching his Bhabhi get so scared. 'The very reason my children come here is because they get to play outside on the full twenty-five acres of land. One time, my youngest said to his mother, "Why don't we have such a big ground to play in?" Just this was enough to make his mother livid and begin beating him, so what if it was our own kid,' he laughed loudly, 'his bloody father is a Lucknavi Sindhi Sain, hahaha!'

Chand Bibi, too, proceeds towards the room inside the haveli, laughing.

'The problem is, Ishaq,' Nawab Mirza's arrow was still aiming at the target, 'That for you, culture is a thing to simply eat, drink, and make merry.'

'But Bhaijaan, you, too, just said something about the taste of culture,' Ishaq Mirza loves provoking his older brother on this topic, 'But anyway, let me tell you the story of my Punjabi neighbour, Fakir Babu. His wife is also a Sindhi. She says, "My man doesn't know anything but when he starts singing Jhule Laalan on the Chimta, Bhai Sain, it's as if the fakir has become a king!" Fakir Babu tells us with so much humility, "She's a crazy Sindhi woman. How would I know how to sing Jhule Laalan very well?" Then he turns to look directly at me, "You know what you can make us do as much as you like, Nawab Ishaq—agriculture. You have to admit, agriculture is the best culture. You who get so easily impressed by any tiny little flower, try holding a cauliflower in your hands. And then smell it. I swear on Allah, you'll start pecking it like a lover's face! No, Bhai Nawab, for Allah's sake, be quiet! You so much as open your mouth, and we get scared that you'll poke ten holes in every single Urdu sentence I utter.' I tell him it should be "every single Urdu sentence we utter", not "I utter". He shoots back, "My man, it's simple! If I'm speaking I'll say, "I utter", if my Sindhi wife is speaking, it'll be "she utters", but our Urdu—no, your Urdu—no, what did you just say? Yeah, *your* Urdu has put such a scare in me that when I'm speaking with a proper Urdu speaker, I forget what I want to say and instead only obsess about speaking proper Urdu. Tell me—what's the use of speaking proper Urdu when it makes you forget what you actually wanted to say?'

'But what are you getting at, Ishaq Mian?'

'Only this, Bhaijaan: what's the point of speaking the language beautifully but repressing what you really want to say? Personally, I have no objection to defiling my language.'

AFTERWORD

Of Bruised Hearts

For years, postcards kept arriving from India; from close relatives, some from others I knew, and then there were postcards from Joginder Paul. I don't recall Joginder-ji ever sending a letter enclosed in an envelope. Now that I sit down to describe his short stories, those postcards float before my eyes.

Joginder Paul belonged to the generation that suffered the trauma of being exiled from their native land, not once but twice. When Pakistan came into being, he and his family wrapped up their life's baggage and left Sialkot for India. But never could he resist looking back at his motherland. Later, to meet the challenges of making a livelihood, he moved to Africa, where he lived for many years, until his yearning for the homeland became unbearable and he returned to India. He established a base, in Aurangabad at first, and then in Delhi, from where he made his final departure, leaving behind an array of exceptional and memorable novels and short stories.

I would visit Joginder Paul in Delhi, and whenever we met, we would share our bruised memories of the cleaving of the country. To write now about his short stories is indeed an honour for me. The scholar-writer of Urdu, Dr Anwaar Ahmad, always referred to Joginder Paul as an 'evergreen old man'. Indeed, evergreen he was, spending his lifetime writing novels such as *Paar Pare* (Beyond Black Waters), *Khwabrau* (Sleepwalkers), *Nadeed* (Blind) and several other creative pieces, each a significant addition to progressive Urdu literature.

During his migration from Sialkot to Ambala in 1947, Joginder Paul witnessed gruesome scenes: violent deaths and tattered corpses scattered everywhere. He saw human beings suddenly turn into enemies of each other. How could he turn his gaze away from the festering dead and their gutted homes? The sorrow of Partition followed his stories everywhere like a shadow.

Sometimes, the dead appeared to come alive in them. At other times, the living were rendered into the dead. He adopted a distinctive writing style whenever he described households. In his story 'Dadiyaan', he writes about an old grandmother, whose house was 'a hundred years older than her,' and in whom we see the reflection of generations of our own grandmothers, who lived in their ancestral homes lost during the partition.

Like millions of people, Joginder Paul, too, grieved forever for the home he had to leave behind. In 'Saans Samundar', he writes, 'One can grow older only in a home. Can those who are homeless ever grow up?' He raises the question that echoes across the border till today: what is a home? A roof under which one lives with one's wife and children—can just that be called a home? No, he writes, home is a place near one's grandparents, whom we can 'easily visit in the graveyard around the corner...'

Partition divided both Bengal and Punjab, and Paul expresses his remorse about the bifurcation of both peoples, and all those around the world: '...two Punjabs, two Chinas, two Vietnams, two Germanies... two worlds...two armies standing against each other in the East and the West.'

He raises many questions regarding human life and its relationships, repeatedly harking back to the role of memory and remembrance, and how these distinguish a human being—all of mankind, sitting on top of the world—from an animal existence. 'If one does not employ one's past for the use of future, how will civilisation progress?' he asks, as he describes the drawing of boundaries and the persistent urge to cross, or else transgress its limits. 'When there are no guards at the border, one remains at home even if it is far away from one's old home,' he writes. But when a member of the family is on this side of the border and it is under strict surveillance, 'it is but natural that one would want to leap to the other side to find out about the other member's well-being'.

In another story, 'Janab-e-Aali', he writes of the desire to leap across borders to meet family members separated during the partition: 'I, after separation of years from my dear ones, I am beginning to feel that they, God forbid, are no more. Those who are dead cannot be met without dying yourself. Therefore, as a very responsible citizen, I think I should adopt the bearing of a professional terrorist and move towards the border and getting shot at from here as well as there, run, leaving my life right there, and land in the lap of my grandmother ... when life itself becomes death, it's better to really die and meet our separated ones ...'

In Joginder Paul's stories, a 'No Man's Land' teems with characters tossed from one shore to the other, friends meet after decades of separation, homes and families are rediscovered, even the gods are lost and found and, often, we lose it all once again. Separated by the division, one was submerged in his beard and his namaaz and the other in the memories of his town on the other side of the border; even the sense of reconciliation with Partition is fraught with doubt and fear. The author writes about a character who has seemingly settled in India, but craves for the lost home in Pakistan: 'Even lost cats and dogs return to their territories one day, wagging their tails. But the man who flies around in aeroplanes all his life, with no place to call his own, loses the connection between his body and his soul.'

Joginder Paul's stories make Partition the butcher's knife with which mankind was assaulted. Irrespective of politics, a human being always longs to embrace his loved ones and his yearning to do so will never end. Joginder-ji had said: 'As a writer I am without an identity of my own or rather the traces of my identity are manifested in all the aspects of the universe. Whatever I see, I am transformed into that...In fact, that is my identity.' I would even say that those who have experienced the trauma of displacement not once but twice confront the danger of losing their identity altogether.

Time plays strange games with humanity and existence. Joginder Paul has enumerated life's losses and sorrows poignantly against a wide variety of backdrops and characters. He is not with us any longer. One is left wondering about the conditions of his third exile...Whatever it is like, one thing I am sure of is that wherever he is, he is busy writing stories about it.

Zahida Hina
October 2019

Translated by Naghma Zafir

Endnotes

1. Mir Taqi Mir, 18th-century Urdu poet.
2. Prayer for the deceased.
3. Deewana meaning 'crazy' or 'obsessed'.

The Translators

Asif Aslam Farrukhi was a Pakistani writer, translator and a literary critic and regular newspaper columnist in Pakistan. He published several books of short fiction as well as translations from Urdu and Sindhi into English. He was also a health expert. He was honoured with the Prime Minister's award for Literature by the Pakistani Academy of Letters. He founded the biannual literary journal, *Dunyazad,* and continued to publish it for nearly twenty years.

Haris Qadeer teaches at the Department of English, University of Delhi, India. He has been a visiting fellow at Co-Futures, University of Oslo (2024), a Charles Wallace India Trust fellow at King's College, London, UK (2022), and a UGC-DAAD visiting fellow at the Department of English, Potsdam University, Germany (2019). His most recent translation includes a co-translation of Premchand's *Karbala* (Sahitya Akademi, 2023). His research articles have appeared in prestigious journals and he has several books to his credit.

Maaz Bin Bilal is an Anglophone poet and a translator working between Hindi-Urdu, English and sometimes Persian. His translations of Mirza Ghalib's Persian masnavi on Banaras as *Temple Lamp,* and of Fikr Taunsvi's Partition days' diary from Urdu as *The Sixth River* have been well-received. He is now translating Mohsin Khan's award-winning novel *Allah Miyan ka Karkhana* from Urdu. Maaz holds a PhD in modern literary studies from Queen's University Belfast and teaches at Jindal Global University.

Mohammad Asim Siddiqui is professor of English at Aligarh Muslim University, India. A critic, translator, and reviewer, his recent publications include *Shahryar* (Sahitya Akademi, 2021), *A History of Aligarh Muslim University 1920-2020* (co-authored, Bennet and Coleman, 2021), *Muslim Identity in Hindi Cinema: Poetics and Politics of Genre and Representation* (Routledge, forthcoming), and translation of *Qurratulain Hyder* (Sahitya Akademi, 2023). His articles and reviews have appeared in many magazines and news portals.

Naghma Zafir retired as an associate professor of English from Zakir Husain Delhi College, University of Delhi. She has translated poetry, stories, and critical articles from Urdu, Hindi and Marathi, published in several noted anthologies and magazines. Recently, she edited a trilingual collection of translated poetry by Bilquis Zafirul Hassan.

Saleem Mir teaches heritage tourism and digital humanities at the Cluster Innovation Centre, University of Delhi. His schooling in Urdu medium has made him deeply passionate for the language. He occasionally writes poetry and believes that translation is crucial for understanding and preserving cultural diversity.

Sami Rafiq is Professor of English at Aligarh Muslim University, India. She is also a translator, author, poet and novelist who has published more than 200 articles, stories and poems in national newspapers and magazines and also several books of translations.Her collection of poems *Woman in the Trees: Poems on Climate and Nature* published in 2022 and her translation of *Farozaan* by Moin Ahsan Jazbi, published in April 2023, are her most recent works.

~

***Translator's Note*:** Haris Qadeer thanks Yusra Iqbal for reviewing the drafts of his translations; Shubham and Aiman Hasney for their help with the translations of 'Fakhtayein' (Doves) and 'Khulabaaz' (Free Spirit); and Aman Nawaz for assisting him with the original Urdu story, 'Bashinde' (The Dwellers).

~

Zahida Hina, author of the Afterword in this collection, is a renowned Pakistani short story writer, novelist, dramatist, essayist, and columnist. As a journalist, she was associated with the daily, *Jang* and the *Daily Express.* She worked extensively with Radio Pakistan, BBC Urdu, and Voice of America. She has been a regular contributor to *Dainik Bhaskar* in India, writing a weekly column, 'Pakistan Diary'. She was nominated for one of the highest awards in Pakistan, 'Pride of Performance', which she declined to accept.

ALSO FROM SPEAKING TIGER

THE SIXTH RIVER

A Journal from the Partition of India

Translated by Maaz Bin Bilal

The Sixth River is the journal Fikr Taunsvi—born Ram Lal Bhatia—wrote from August to November 1947 as Lahore disintegrated around him. His identity reduced, overnight, merely to a Hindu in his beloved and cosmopolitan city, he is angry at the shortsightedness and ineptness of Radcliffe, Nehru, Gandhi and Jinnah. In the company of likeminded friends such as the poet Sahir Ludhianvi, he mourns the loss of the art and culture of Lahore in the bloodlust and deluded euphoria of freedom. He is bewildered when old friends suddenly turn staunch nationalists and advise him to either convert or leave the newly created country. And then the unspeakable trauma that millions are facing during Partition reaches Fikr's doorstep when a neighbour murders his daughter, and he is eventually forced to migrate to Amritsar in India.

ALSO FROM SPEAKING TIGER

SONG OF OUR SWAMPLAND

Manzu Islam

When news arrives of the killings in Dhaka, the villagers know that the army from West Pakistan will soon be in their area. But unlike the other young men, and his beloved step-sister Moni Banu, Kamal cannot join the resistance. Born with a hole for a mouth, everyone—except Abbas Miah, the teacher who adopts him, and Moni Banu and a few friends—regards him as the village idiot. But it is he who will see the truths that others will not or cannot see.

When hundreds of villagers are slaughtered, Abbas Miah and Kamal embark on a Noah's Ark journey in a boat, with a motley group of survivors, to find refuge in the distant floodplains until the war is over. But there can be no escape from the war and the issues it raises.

As our guide to the painful emergence of the new nation of Bangladesh, Kamal is forced both to observe the face of evil and look within to discover whether he has the capacity for true community and forgiveness.

ALSO FROM SPEAKING TIGER

UNPARTITIONED TIME

A Daughter's Story

Malavika Rajkotia

Jindo, Malavika Rajkotia's father, arrives in India as the Partition riots erupt. He is given a patch of barren land in small-town Karnal, to clear, cultivate, and resume life as landlord and patriarch. But stripped of his history, and facing an uncertain future in a land with an unfamiliar language, he transforms profoundly. Around this generous, funny, loving, and growingly despondent figure, Rajkotia weaves an intricate narrative of her family's past and present, exploring themes of longing and belonging, privilege and the loss of it, and reflecting on the resilience of a people denied autonomy. Through her raw, lyrical prose, she guides readers through the struggles of a sprawling clan—uncles, aunts, siblings, cousins, and revered heroes—striving for recognition, identity, and security.

Rajkotia fearlessly confronts her milieu, whether navigating the radical Khalistan movement, the tensions between the Sikh faith and Hindu nationalism, or the pervasive cynicism of Indian politics. Her vivid, meditative, finely-detailed portraits of a rich family life are filled with moments of tears, laughter, and music, and a diverse array of characters who are immensely relatable. Ultimately, this brave and moving book is about the enduring quest for meaning and fulfilment that transcends cultural boundaries.

UNPARTITIONED TIME